LAST STAND

"I'll start on the right!" Justin Ross yelled. "Sewell, you start on the left. And Collins, you take out as many in the middle as you can!"

"I'm down to my last five rounds, Justin!" cried Collins.

"Then I wanna see *five* Commie heads roll!" Ross shot back angrily. He took in a breath, held it, then slowly squeezed the trigger until the weapon bucked and a charging NVA soldier on the far side of the clearing was catapulted backward off his feet.

"Lucky shot, Justin," Sewell laughed. It was the sort of helpless chuckle men release when they know they're doomed and there's nothing they can do about it.

Collins pulled his trigger five times, and three Vietnamese belly-flopped into the muck, screaming their lives up at the starry night. "That's it, guys!" His tone was apologetic. "My cookie jar's empty."

"Mine, too," admitted Ross.

Then the NVA troops came storming at them through the darkness. . . .

THE SURVIVALIST SERIES
by Jerry Ahern

#1: TOTAL WAR (960, $2.50)
The first in the shocking series that follows the unrelenting search for ex-CIA covert operations officer John Thomas Rourke to locate his missing family—after the button is pressed, the missiles launched and the multimegaton bombs unleashed. . . .

#2: THE NIGHTMARE BEGINS (810, $2.50)
After WW III, the United States is just a memory. But ex-CIA covert operations officer Rourke hasn't forgotten his family. While hiding from the Soviet forces, he adheres to his search!

#3: THE QUEST (851, $2.50)
Not even a deadly game of intrigue within the Soviet High Command, and a highly placed traitor in the U.S. government can deter Rourke from continuing his desperate search for his family.

#4: THE DOOMSAYER (893, $2.50)
The most massive earthquake in history is only hours away, and Communist-Cuban troops, Soviet-Cuban rivalry, and a traitor in the inner circle of U.S. II block Rourke's path.

#5: THE WEB (1145, $2.50)
Blizzards rage around Rourke as he picks up the trail of his family and is forced to take shelter in a strangely quiet Tennessee valley town. But the quiet isn't going to last for long!

#6: THE SAVAGE HORDE (1243, $2.50)
Rourke's search gets sidetracked when he's forced to help a military unit locate a cache of eighty megaton warhead missiles hidden on the New West Coast—and accessible only by submarine!

#7: THE PROPHET (1339, $2.50)
As six nuclear missiles are poised to start the ultimate conflagration, Rourke's constant quest becomes a desperate mission to save both his family and all humanity from being blasted into extinction!

#8: THE END IS COMING (1374, $2.50)
Rourke must smash through Russian patrols and cut to the heart of a KGB plot that could spawn a lasting legacy of evil. And when the sky bursts into flames, consuming every living being on the planet, it will be the ultimate test for THE SURVIVALIST.

Available wherever paperbacks are sold, or order direct from the Publisher. Send cover price plus 50¢ per copy for mailing and handling to Zebra Books, Dept. 1647, 475 Park Avenue South, New York, N.Y. 10016. DO NOT SEND CASH.

NIK-UHERNIK

WAR DOGS
#3
BUSTING CAPS

ZEBRA BOOKS
KENSINGTON PUBLISHING CORP.

ZEBRA BOOKS

are published by

Kensington Publishing Corp.
475 Park Avenue South
New York, NY 10016

Copyright © 1985 by Nik-Uhernik

All rights reserved. No part of this book may be reproduced in any form or by any means without the prior written consent of the Publisher, excepting brief quotes used in reviews.

First printing: August 1985

Printed in the United States of America

*For Mark, Dennis, Tim and Brian.
And for Leslie, rose among the thorns.*

Americans are big boys. You can talk them into almost anything. All you have to do is sit with them for half an hour over a bottle of whiskey and be a nice guy . . .

—South Vietnamese Premier Nguyen Cao Ky,
July 1965

You should never believe a Vietnamese. He's not like you. He's an Asiatic. The Vietnamese of today has seen too much dishonesty, too much maneuvering, and he doesn't believe in anything any more. He automatically thinks he's got to camouflage himself. He doesn't dare tell the truth any more because too often it brings him unhappiness. What's the point of telling the truth?

—South Vietnamese Premier Nguyen Cao Ky,
July 1965

If I could write a poem, it would be something about how impossible it is to hold sunshine in your arms, but how warm and good the sunshine makes you feel when you try.

—John Cassidy, *A Station In The Delta*

Yellow gold is plentiful, compared to white-haired friends.

—Robert Daley, *Year Of The Golden Dragon*

PROLOGUE

Korea, 1950 . . .

As if in a dream—his mind numb, his reactions alien—Chandler watched the brown combat boots moving slowly back and forth below him, plowing the snow aside, stumbling now and then across roots protruding from the barren, crater-pocked hillside. He knew the boots belonged to him, that *his* feet were guiding them along, that *he* was somehow directing his course through the blinding blizzard. But he had lost all feeling in his toes sometime before dawn, and to help pass the time his mind had begun to laugh down at the seemingly unattached feet as he floated along above them, in awe of their ability to endure, to trudge on without him. *Feet, do yo thing!* he giggled to himself.

Bent over now, like some prehistoric cave man in a helmet, Chandler drooped his left shoulder slightly, shifting the weight of the wounded man on his back. Without the slightest command, the boots came to a casual halt. And after the bulk of the two-hundred-pound black infantryman had settled across a new spot, making Chandler more comfortable, at least temporarily, the boots magically resumed their unprotesting march along the narrow trail.

Chandler tensed his fingers until he could feel the stock of the carbine; his hands had also been growing numb lately, and he constantly checked and double-checked to insure he had not dropped his weapon somewhere along the trail. Not that it would have mattered that much: the rifle was empty.

The edges of his eyes frozen with moisture, he glanced around suspiciously as a large bird took to the air upon detecting his approach. Instinctively, he raised the rifle, defensively, to his waist as he scanned the charred and broken tree stumps cluttering the hillside below the trail—you couldn't be too careful—*the ChiComs were everywhere!* Even so close to camp. There were no longer any front lines in the war. The camp he was returning to was a couple klicks south of the DMZ, but with the enemy all the way south to Inchon and beyond, territorial games meant nothing. Not until the fat, grey turtledove was a hundred yards away, a mere speck against the white sky, did he spot it. Suddenly depressed, Chandler lowered his rifle, painfully aware he had just let warm food escape between his hands.

He scratched at the stubble on his chin, feeling the caked blood in the whiskers. He ran his fingers up into his mustache. Chips of dried blood fell away, fluttering down onto the snowdrifts.

The way his mustache was caked with frozen blood reminded him of those days in his youth when he'd hiked through the snow-blanketed mountains of

Montana with his friends, searching for women. Indian maidens who didn't really exist—except in his own mind, and those of his lonely high school pals. The girls in class were so boring, so . . . predictable. Nothing like the Comanche and Cherokee warrior women in the novels that his buddies had devoured faster than the publisher could put them out.

Back then, so long ago it now seemed, Chad had run with a pack of seven or eight close friends. They'd all lived in a cramped half-square-mile housing project which was home to blue-collar loggers and white-collar naturalists. Directly in the center of the modestly priced oak-wood homes there'd been a vast, sprawling vacant field, which was divided up, mazelike, by a haphazard network of wild hedges and thick man-high trunks. It was where they'd built their underground clubhouse. Where they'd met after dark to discuss the novels, the authors' backgrounds, the possibility of hidden meanings or clues, and the chance their favorite novels were not fiction at all, but treasure maps to paradise and—

"Let's hustle it up a little, Chad!" the soldier behind him muttered, invading his thoughts without warning.

Chandler glanced back at the fellow paratrooper and nodded, then checked his feet; they were still trudging along, unintimidated. He wondered what the other man was complaining about. They were almost home now, if you could call Camp Starburst home. Nevertheless, he mentally commanded his boots to expedite their little dance. Another flake of blood fluttered down from his mustache, to be immediately plowed under by his feet, and he returned to the mountains and blue skies of Montana again.

He saw his friends battling the blizzards to reach the highest peaks in the dead of winter (for surely you could not find paradise without first enduring great hardship and suffering); those who could grow mustaches saw the weather coat them first with frost, then layers of their own breath, until halfway through the hike their upper lips became heavy horizontal icicles, more than one of his buddies remarking that it seemed they were re-enacting a Jack London Yukon novel instead. Chad could still remember how the remarks had caused him to grin: London's tales were dog stories. And their expeditions up into the high valleys of Montana hadn't turned up *any* women. Beautiful *or* ugly.

A soft, drawn-out moan from one of the wounded soldiers drifted up to Chandler, and he glanced back again at the survivors of his squad. Beyond the last man he could see they were leaving a bloody trail in the bone-white snow. But it couldn't be helped. They were lucky enough to be alive. None of them had the extra reserves of energy it would have taken to execute a proper extraction from the field, wiping fresh snow over the blood. Hopefully, the wind and the drifts would handle that problem for them. Also, the men's instincts were very much alive, and none of them "felt" the enemy pursuing them from the site of the counterambush, miles and lifetimes back. Or perhaps it was just that none of them cared any longer.

Chandler ran his fingers along the scalp wound a half-inch below the hairline. The temperature and the wind had curbed the bleeding. He squeezed his left cheek slightly, until the pain bit back at him, reassuring him he still had *some* feeling in his system. The Chinese infantryman had butt-stroked him there with a carbine; Chad would never forget the look in the man's startled eyes an instant before Chandler had plunged his bayonet through the Asian's throat.

Almost routinely, he reached up without looking and probed the throat of the American lying limply across his back. He was almost disappointed when he found the weak pulse—so great was his own pain now . . . his own despair. Chandler wasn't about to waste the energy carrying a stiff, but as long as the soldier clung to life, Chandler would try to keep him from cold death; he would not surrender another American life to the Land of the Morning Calm, as the Koreans called this moonscape of misery and destruction.

The voices in his mind laughed down at Chad Chandler as he trudged relentlessly through the blizzard. They were the voices of memory, more than anything: a grinning recruiter, who couldn't believe a genuine high-school graduate was *volunteering* to cast off to a war that was half a world away; the giggling girls from study hall—where they'd never studied, but had thrown firecrackers and snowballs, and left tacks on the teachers' seats—who'd slobbered over his fancy uniform after he'd coasted through boot camp; the old gunny sergeant, retired of course, who'd lived down the street and had bought Chad his first beers in exchange for listening to him slur through his the-women-in-the-Orient-are-the-most-exotic-by-far sea stories. Yes, they're more beautiful, more obedient, more mysterious than the round-eyed women we have to endure here, he'd proclaimed. You're doing the right thing, son ... join the military and see how they love and live on the other side of the globe ... it'll wake you up.

But he had not found his paradise maidens waiting for him in Korea, either. The mountains were more violent and hostile than any in Montana, and the only breasts he saw were in torn and folded *Playboys*. ...

"How much farther?" the voice drifted into his thoughts, interrupting the memories again.

Chandler glanced back. The soldier directly behind him had spoken this time. "Not much," he whispered back hoarsely, his throat aching. "Less than a half-klick, Johnny ... less than a half-klick...."

"Fuck this, Chad...." came the soft response. "Fuck this shit...."

Yah, I know, he thought, keeping silent. Fuck it all. The training, the pep talks, the mission.... They all knew nobody really gave a damn if they made it out of Indian territory or not. Who really knew where they were or what they were doing, anyway? Surely not family or close friends—who were the people who *would* care, the only ones who *would* appreciate all the suffering and sacrifice. But this was just another of those secret, eyes-and-ears-only, deny-access-to-the-press, fuck-if-I-know-what-you're-talking-about-ma'am missions of madness nobody above the rank of colonel was ever told about. Chandler knew the stuffy congressmen back in the States and the schmucks in the Senate were lounging around their fireplaces, getting skull jobs while they sipped fine brandy, totally oblivious to what his squad—most of them—had just survived.

Andrews, Cartwright, and Jackson had died instantly, taking the brunt of the antipersonnel mines and automatic weapons fire as the nine Americans had begun to venture into enemy territory, en route to attempt the kidnapping of a high-ranking Communist field commander. Sloop and Withers had taken a lot of shrapnel, and had sustained belly wounds besides, but at least they were still drifting in and out of consciousness. Young Corporal Pruitt—Johnny to his few battlefield friends—was carrying Sloop, and had received only a minor bullet graze across one cheek. Behind him, Private Franky "Switchblade" Martinez struggled along through the snow with a black soldier nearly twice his size across his shoulders.

The trooper across Chad's own back was, for all intents and purposes, brain dead, but as long as a pulse haunted him, Chandler would struggle through the blizzard with the helpless man. Each time the wind bit deep and the cold slashed through his clothes like scissors of ice, he fought the urge to just dump the man, thinking instead: *what if it was me, in his place.* And down deep in his gut, he knew Parks would do the same for him till his energy was sapped.

As they started up the last hill, Chad found himself thinking more and more about the mission itself. Not the way their field radio had malfunctioned halfway to the kill zone, nor the way a map issued to the squad moments before deployment had turned out to be totally useless because of its inaccuracies. Not even how most of their weapons had begun misfiring when they were caught in an unexpected counterambush five miles before even reaching what was considered Indian territory. Those were mere unfortunates. They could all be explained away with little or no effort on the part of the command staff. What really bothered Chandler was the look that had been in the lieutenant's eyes as he gave the briefing prior to field immersion. Or, rather, the manner in which he had gone out of his way to avoid looking Chad's men in the eyes. Like he was sending them all to their deaths . . . to their *executions*. But without any warning. Without even a last cigarette.

It didn't make sense, he argued with himself. It was not as if he headed some elite commando unit. They were but one of hundreds of such highly trained, carefully screened paratrooper squads.

Chandler logged a mental note to confront the young, baby-faced lieutenant once they were safely back inside the wire.

When he rounded the bend in the trail that brought them within sight of the camp, Chandler held up his hand suddenly. The others didn't even notice the silent command, and they bumped into him from behind. Tortured groans, like muffled gasps in a nightmare, drifted along on the brittle air, as wounds were ground against wounds. But everyone kept their balance; none of them tumbled into the drifts.

"What is it?" Switchblade muttered, his eyes glued to his boots, amazed they had not stumbled over each other. The weight across his shoulders, and the fatigue, prevented him from looking up.

"I feel it, too," Pruitt cut in, forcing his face up against the frozen creases across the back of his neck. "Something's . . . not . . . right. . . ."

At first, it appeared the camp had been plucked from the white wasteland while they were gone. A few utility poles, ramrod straight yet shifting about in the haze, pierced up through the flurries, and the silver loops of sharp concertina wire sparkled back at them through the brilliant expanses of gleaming snowdrifts—but at first they could see none of the Camp Starburst quonset huts. Then, like some arctic mirage, the winds drifted down from the hilltops to part the walls of floating white mist, and they could make out the armory and the temporary command post, and even the mess tent.

"I feel there's . . . I feel there's someone up in the hills," Pruitt expounded. "Watching . . . waiting. . . ."

Chandler felt he should swallow, but his throat was too dry, and after he realized he was orchestrating gut responses, the effort seemed foolish and he shifted his concentration.

His weary eyes focused on a guard tower rising along the east perimeter fence line. It appeared abandoned, but that didn't really mean anything. Show your face in this land, and you'd never hear the shot that split your nostrils apart.

"So we gonna wait here all fucking day, Chad?" Switchblade shifted the dead weight about on his shoulders, then persuaded his feet to do a little dance—just to assure him they were still responsive to his commands. The boots ignored him.

Chandler didn't immediately answer as he analyzed his own instincts. *It's not somebody watching, it's the gut fear of desolation . . . of desertion. . . .* He ground his teeth together silently, wishing they still had their radio: without it, receiving and returning the password challenge would be more than dangerous . . . it could be deadly.

He would have to opt for the next best thing. The way the old timers had done it in the past. The method they swore was better than any modern, newfangled radio-electronic contraption. Chandler pulled the metal Halloween cricket from the empty ammo pouch on his belt.

They were about fifty yards from the perimeter bunkers. Though the land was lit with a surrealistic haze because of the snowfall and howling wind, sunrise was four hours behind them, and the guard towers would be unmanned. The sentries would be in the ground bunker. They were probably staring out at him right now, on the verge of going snowblind.

Chandler gave the small cricket three quick snaps

with his thumb and forefinger. Then he waited, ear cocked against the raging storm, but he heard nothing in response above the sound of the wind.

"Nothing. . . ." Switchblade was still staring at the ground, but his ears, too, were perked in the direction of the military compound.

The feelings of abandonment began drifting in on Chandler again. There was no sign of activity anywhere on the post, but it *was* the weekend, and even though this was a combat zone, the men not assigned to guard duty or field patrols were probably still snugly nestled deep inside their racked sleeping bags.

"One of us gotta low-crawl up there halfway and announce ourselves," Pruitt finally said, his own eyes appearing lifeless and dazed as they scanned the installation from one end to the other.

"And you's hereby elected," added Switchblade sarcastically, though his tone was matter-of-fact and unaccusing.

"Watch over him," Chandler said as he gently laid the soldier he had been carrying against a snowdrift, wrapped his poncho around the upper part of his body, then checked for a pulse one last time.

"Watch your ass, Chad," Pruitt warned without shifting his gaze. "Somethin' smells powerful bad about the arrangement we're walking into . . . powerful bad, friend."

A few minutes later, the frostbitten paratrooper was halfway between the camp and the men from his patrol. He allowed himself time to inspect the perimeter again, and finding no new signs of life, snapped the metal cricket three more times.

The wind howled back in response, and the wet snow, like tiny razors, stung at his face, unable to cut yet producing a sensation like countless minute hatchets attacking his skin.

Chandler advanced a few more feet, then halted abruptly as his ankle caught a hidden tripwire, invisible in the snow. It was a miracle he had not detonated the mine, and after cautiously detaching himself from it, considered just yelling out his arrival, hoping for the best. But the Americans had all been briefed about that long ago: the North Koreans had speech specialists who, especially under these inclement conditions, could imitate a caucasian's tone pattern precisely. The rules were strict—all parties wishing access through the perimeter had to sound the password. Popping up for a visual inspection was unhealthy; tower guards were notorious for shooting at anything that moved and asking questions later. Bunker rats were worse.

Chandler snapped the cricket again three times. The metallic noise should alert the guard to his presence, then a challenge would be voiced from the other side of the barbed wire.

He knew the password for this twenty-four-hour period was *seven*. The sentry would give a number, such as ten. Chandler would have to respond with three, or, in general, that number which when subtracted from whatever number the guard yelled would make seven. The man behind the concertina could give any number he wanted. The respondent wishing access to the compound had only a few seconds to respond *correctly*. Otherwise, every piece of artillery within a five-mile radius would be brought to bear on the tiny slice of war-zone real estate where the intruder's voice had come from.

Chandler snapped the metal cricket three more times, waiting for a lull between wind gusts. Snow tried to bury him where he lay.

Three identical clicks answered him from somewhere in the distance; the storm made an exact location impossible to determine. He hesitated, worrying he was hearing only an echo or a manifestation of the blizzard, but he knew that was unlikely. Wasting no more time, he responded with four clicks. The sentry should have given more than seven clicks, or a verbal number higher than seven. Instead, it appeared the challenge was being given in reverse—something that would quickly trip up a soldier with little skill at simple math—a practice which was dangerous under wartime conditions. Games were for the National Guard and the weekend warriors.

The white wind kicked up again, and at the same time a voice, barely audible, called out to him from the direction of the camp. He could not make out the words . . . were they *advance and be recognized*?, the classic secondary challenge.

"Chandler!" he yelled back. "Bravo Company, Niner squad . . . be sure and deactivate your perimeter! I got walking wounded coming in!"

The unintelligible voice, like a ghost on the wind, answered him again, and Chandler waved back at his men to follow him, then started toward the fence line.

Despite the freezing wind, hairs began to rise on the back of Chandler's neck as he grew closer the compound. The sentries had now had more than ample time to identify him visually, but he was unable to spot anyone along the perimeter—not even any bobbing helmets as they rushed along the trench for a better vantage point.

He glanced back over his shoulder; Switchblade and Pruitt, already bent over with their burdens, now carried Chandler's charge between them. He grinned inwardly, nodding his head proudly.

Less than a minute later, he was crawling over the last slope toward the perimeter trench line, in the direction he knew the early-morning sentries always congregated to nurse their mugs of brew, where the wind was less harsh.

"Friendlies!" he announced, after removing his helmet and cautiously poking his head above the rim of the bunker.

At first, Chandler thought he had happened upon another ambush site. Below him, an American soldier lay on his back across a tarp, his head cushioned by a helmet with a jacket wrapped around it. He appeared dead to the world. But there was no blood.

Chandler glanced back and forth, down both lengths of the narrow but deep trench. There were no other infantrymen visible.

Why you son of a bitch! he thought. He gritted his teeth and swung his legs over the edge of the bunker, landing on his feet beside the sleeping guard.

The private, startled by the sudden motion around

him and Chandler's boots landing within a foot of his head, rolled to the side and dove for the antipersonnel mines panel half-buried in the opposite wall of the trench.

"*No!*" Chandler called out at the top of his lungs, but the sentry, still half asleep, was already grabbing the detonator and twisting the tiny metal dynamo.

Chandler leaped onto the man, but he was not quick enough.

The air all around erupted with a long drawn-out screech as multiple explosions along the perimeter sent hot, smoking metal arcing out in all directions, tearing through the storm. The wind howled back in response, unimpressed with the show of force.

"You fool!" Chandler slammed his fist against the side of the private's face, fracturing the upper jaw. The paratrooper's ring tore a deep gash across the smaller soldier's left cheek, and blood sprayed across the snow at their feet.

Chandler, one hand still grasping the private's throat, froze in the middle of another swing, his ears picking through the sounds of the storm, but he couldn't hear even one scream. He was familiar with the mines placed along the perimeter of Camp Starburst—his men were the ones who had implemented the compound's defenses. He knew the firepower that had just been unleashed with a simple surge of electricity was double that needed to wipe out a battalion of alert enemy soldiers—but only five unprepared men had gone up against it, expecting nothing at the wire but muffled attaboys and strong cups of army coffee to chase away the frostbite.

The soldier beneath him was trying to say something, but Chandler still had his throat squeezed tightly shut; whether it was an excuse, an apology, or outright rage, Chad didn't care. He kept a tight grip, fighting off the urge to slam his fist into the man's face one last time.

Then his ears picked up the noise. Far off . . . beyond the wire, down across the hill where he had last seen his squad before they were cut down. A low, agonized moan, laced with extreme pain.

Chandler released the sentry and rose to one knee.

"I didn't know!" the sentry cried. "I thought you were one of them damn Chinamen—"

"Shut up!" Chandler commanded, ears perked again as he frowned at the angry antics of the snowstorm.

"I swear . . . I thought—"

Chandler lashed out with a boot, making contact against the splintered jaw. Screaming, the sentry slammed back off his haunches onto his side, cupping his wound in his hand. "Be *silent*!" Chandler was incensed as he reached down and picked up the man's carbine. "You're already in enough trouble as it is, *mister*!"

He braced his head against the wind again, searching for the sounds, but now there was only the laughter of the blizzard as it ran its icy fingers through his hair.

Chandler started back up the steep slope to the top of the trench, now ignoring the soldier.

"You shoulda gave the password!" the sentry snapped back, both hurt and dismay in his worried expression. He was feeling the side of his face for deformities, feeling little pain because of the cold.

Chandler halted just below the rim of the trench line and looked back down at the man. "What?" he asked incredulously.

"You shoulda challenged me first!" The sentry sounded more brave and confident now. "None of this woulda happened if you'd of just identified yourselves!" he seemed to rationalize, forcing from his mind any memory that he had just been sleeping on duty. "You Recon dudes always crawlin' about sneakin' up on people . . . we all knew someday somethin' *bad* like this was gonna go down. . . ."

Chandler thought back to the cricket clicks he had heard, and the voice yelling above the fury of the storm. Starting back up over the lip of the trench, he took his eyes from the sentry's while asking both himself and the other soldier, "But if it wasn't you . . ."

Screaming war cries pierced through the howling wind as Chandler pulled himself above the trench wall in time to see the wave of angry Chinese soldiers cresting against the perimeter wire.

"Aw, fuck!" His throat went painfully dry, prohibiting him from swallowing as he brought the carbine up to his shoulder. Already, enemy infantrymen wearing padded uniforms were diving onto the razor-sharp concertina, pulling the strands as close together as possible while their comrades raced across their backs, entering the compound.

Chandler chambered a round into the bolt-action rifle and took aim on two men raising a long ladder against the highest portion of the fence line, but a sudden shower of lead directed at the bunker wall sent dirt clods and metal slivers flying about at all angles, and he toppled backward, onto the already dazed sentry.

"Say yo' prayers, brother!" said the sentry. His face in the mud and snow beneath him, he sensed what was happening and appeared to have already accepted his fate. "Judgement Day has arrived!"

"Not if Chad Chandler has anything to say about it, *brother*!" Chad responded, pulling the bayonet from his belt and twisting it into place. "Get on that damn field phone and send out the alarm!"

Then he waited, rifle stock against his shoulder, front sights pointed up at the lip of the trench. He sat on his haunches, Oriental fashion, in the bottom of the dark pit, waiting. Listening to the sentry's boots fade in the distance as he ran for the field phone. Waiting. Well aware this just might be it. The end. The grand finale. Or as the Asians said simply: *fini*. But what a glorious conclusion to his adventure in this life!

Chandler had accepted Death long ago. If one was going to remain in this occupation, he had to come to terms with the other world at a young age. *A soldier is granted the privilege of determining the place and time and circumstances of his death....* He'd be damned if he'd fizzle out like some candle extinguished by a night breeze—he'd bid Mother Earth farewell like a falling star!

Chandler put on his best hellish grin as he began to feel the muffled rumble in the walls of dirt rising up all around him—the crescendo of a thousand boots running toward his location. At peace with fate, he felt his hearbeat subside, despite the adrenalin rush. He began to depress the rifle's trigger as he heard their voices now, growing ever nearer, and he forced the edges of his demonic smile up even farther—finally prepared to kiss Lady Death on the lips.

But first, he would take as many of the Chinese bastards along with him as possible.

1.

Cambodia. Thirteen years later. . . .

The huge panther sat on her haunches, unmoving except for glowing green eyes that slowly shifted about, following the red and yellow embers that also glowed as they floated about on the warm night breeze. Resting on a steep hilltop, several valleys below her jungle lair, the powerful cat produced a continuous throaty growl, controlled yet wild, as she gazed down on the campfires a quarter-mile away. The agile beast, her belly full, was not restless as she watched the frolicking humans, but appeared content.

For the moment.

A blue dragonfly, mischievous and the length of a good cigar, descended from the triple canopy obscuring the stars and landed on the panther's shoulder, but the animal didn't seem to notice as one ear twitched forward and her eyes suddenly narrowed, locking onto a small group of the humans that had abruptly grabbed one of their own and were now dragging him over to the edge of a peaceful lagoon. Odd, how both the laughter and screaming increased with the unpredicted yet acceptable event.

The big cat lowered herself into the prone position, deeper within the cover of fallen palm fronds, as the noise from below increased and a new bonfire sent more sparks against the darkness. But the creature felt no fear—only caution.

Her instincts told the panther to retreat back up into the heights of the rolling hills that overlooked the valley floor, but she remained where she was, intrigued by all the activity in this stretch of jungle which was usually so black and silent after the sun fell and the birds and monkeys went to sleep.

She draped a heavy paw across the other, then lowered her massive jaws onto the fur, throat still rumbling quietly. Her eyes watched the loud, two-legged creatures far below, and she licked her chops once in anticipation, leg muscles tensing as the dancing and music reached a dramatic pitch, but she stayed where she was after that. Unmoving. Silent as death. Waiting patiently.

Except for her green, glowing eyes.

Justin Ross glanced at his watch, then scratched his mustache slightly, as if the gesture would help hide his smile.

"Let go of me, you mothers—"

Young Cory MacArthur's protest was cut short as Sewell and Collins counted off the third swing and threw him face-first into the murky lagoon.

Ross felt a slight laugh rise in his throat, but he suppressed it, remaining totally silent as his wary eyes lost their twinkle when they started following the three slender women in sarongs.

In their late teens, the Cambodians were all filling out quite nicely—especially for jungle dwellers—and the girl in the lead gave Justin a shy wink before looking quickly away. All three carried large platters atop their heads. The metal dishes, thin and intricately decorated, carried bottles of rice wine and fresh fruit from the rain forests beyond the valley.

Ross's eyes fell a foot or so as he concentrated on the tightly wrapped breasts bouncing along with each graceful footfall. The drums beating in his ears were beginning to make his blood boil, and that surprised him, for although this night had been set aside for a celebration feast, he hadn't planned on wasting energy lusting after the native maidens.

The last girl in the convoy had a particularly sensual manner of swishing her hips as she walked, but the maneuver was not enough to keep Ross's attention as the three passed between the bonfires—his eyes stopped on Chad Chandler, who was all alone, nursing a mug of Vietnamese beer.

The ex-paratrooper, ex-mercenary, ex-convict had been sociable enough when the feast first began, but once the young tribesmen had lit the circle of bonfires to chase away the night, Chandler had melted away from the others, finding himself a private little spot where he would be out of the main swirl of festivities.

He had been staring into the flames, trancelike, ever since. . . .

"Payback is a bitch, you assholes!" Cory had surfaced in a geyser of lagoon spray and tangled mosses, a crayfish ten inches long in one hand. He threw the slimy thing at Collins and started for shore, then abruptly changed his mind, and tore off his shirt.

Motioning for of the closest Cambodian women to join him, he fell back into the high ripples, arms straight out from his sides, and began floating on his back, toward the center of the lagoon. Several girls pulled the knot from between their breasts, letting their sarongs drop around their ankles, then smoothly stepped out of them and dove after the American teenager.

"Cherry-boy's finally gonna get some!" Collins smiled brightly over at Sewell as they watched the dozen crescent moons arc out from the banks of the lagoon and disappear beneath the surface. The splashing water was illuminated by the campfires, and it looked like silver slivers of tinsel thrown out against the black of midnight.

The giggling girls finally caught Cory's attention again. Startled by their overwhelming numbers, his head popped up, his eyes went wide, and he flopped over onto his stomach awkwardly and began swimming frantically away from them.

"What a pussy!" Sewell called out.

"What a *lotta* pussy!" Collins countered, his grin ear to ear now.

"I was talking about Mac," Sewell replied, then lost his smile as he frowned deeply for Brent's benefit.

Justin Ross whirled around as his shoulder was touched from behind, but his own grin remained firmly in place.

"Ah . . . my Justin . . ." said a tall, dark-complected woman with high cheekbones, serious eyes, and jet-black hair meticulously braided atop her head, as she bent forward and poured liquid from a copper flask into Ross's mug. "You would like some more—"

"Enough, enough, Princess," he managed as he started to rise, fighting the urge to stare at the firm, upturned breasts barely restrained by the sarong's thin fabric. He was shocked she would serve him instead of having one of the servants do it. But, then again, he was coming to learn that this tribe considered all its members equal, and that royalty, revered as it was by instinct, was still acknowledged by all present to be merely an accident of birth.

"No . . . sit," she commanded gently, pressing the flask to his mug so that to resist would mean spilling the wine.

"I am honored you would—" he began, but she silenced him by placing the fingers of her free hand against his lips.

"Quiet," she said, sitting on the mat beside him. Ross became uneasy and somewhat irritated as he sensed her bodyguards close-by, lurking behind the tall lagoon reeds. "Enjoy. . . ."

"Your people here really know how to party," he laughed lightly, instantly regretting the choice of words. The princess would not notice, but Ross himself disdained plastic social pleasantries.

"It is not often I have returned to me a brother I feared was lost from my people forever," she said, praise and thanks again in her tone, as it had been all day.

"We only liberated an innocent man from unlawful detention," he replied, his smile now matching hers. He shifted his submachine gun away from his thigh so he could get more comfortable and at the same time allow her more room.

"My brother has this bad habit of dabbling in the unknown, gambling against unreasonable odds, and seeking adventure beyond his means," she said sadly, nodding her head from side to side. "Hopefully this will teach him a lesson. . . ."

"If it's excitement he's after," Ross waved his hand out at the ominous shadows in the night they both knew were low valley peaks, "I'm sure the creatures of the jungle out there would be glad to accommodate him . . . one on one. . . ."

"Our community has five women for each man," she revealed; Ross knew the numbers were the result of years of war between clans, the authorities, and the communists. "But do you think he would be content with the pursuit of one young maiden?" "No!" she answered her own question.

"He is young." Ross was not sure why he came to the young man's defense—this latest escapade had nearly cost all of them their lives.

"He is foolish!" she snapped loudly, like the embers crackling in a nearby campfire.

"Foolish," Ross repeated the word softly, not really agreeing, as he thought back on past misadventures.

"And stubborn!" She set down the flask and waved a tiny fist at a rare star that appeared briefly in a break in the dense triple canopy of vegetation overhead.

Stubborn, he thought, glancing over at Chandler. The man was still staring into the tall, licking flames. Ross wondered what the former mercenary could possibly be thinking about. The last mission to Saigon? Or maybe something from deeper within his past, something Ross doubted he would ever hear about.

"How much longer can I count on you staying with us?" the princess murmured as she pressed his forearm gently. "I wish so much," she glanced around for the first time to see if anyone was within earshot, "your people might remain indefinitely. . . . Khmer women make excellent wives, you know." She did not move closer to him, as Ross wanted her to. He searched the depths of her eyes for an answer to the puzzle he had been piecing together all week, but as ever they were too dark for him to find what he sought. She stared through him at times, and her expression was always a collage of emotions too complex for him to decipher. And he had never wanted to sleep with a woman so much in his life.

"We are soldiers." Ross swallowed his desires and looked away. "Soon, we must be moving on. . . ."

"You do not like Svay Rieng valley?" she asked, and shifted her expression to mild insult and hurt though she knew he could see through it.

"I do not have total control over—" he began to make excuses, but her slender hand sliced the air between them, cutting him off.

"You are the boss," her tone remained soft.

"But I am not the *big* boss," he smiled, taking her hand in both of his and lightly kissing it. "Lord knows I wish I made the decisions around here. . . ."

"Then how long have we the pleasure of your company?" She made a disappointed face and jerked her hand away.

"A few days," he said, almost bitterly. "A few days, at most."

She motioned toward his weapon. "Your supply of ammunition has been sorely depleted by this . . . courtesy you have extended my people." She reached forward and ran her fingers along the cool barrel of the gun. Ross felt himself growing hard, and he tried to concentrate on decapitated corpses without missing any of her words. The effort, awkward and unnatural, nearly made him laugh out loud. "I shall make sure the protectors compensate you." She shifted to examining the belt of rounds hanging from the loop over his left shoulder. "We may not have the appropriate caliber you require. If not, I shall see you are outfitted with an entirely new arsenal. . . ."

"Not necessary, Princess." There he went, mildly protesting again, she thought, silencing him with two fingers against his lips.

"Raina," she said. It was the name she always asked him and the others to call her by. Ross knew it was not Cambodian; it was probably something she had adopted from her years abroad, studying in Paris, before the province had fallen on hard times, and her parents had disappeared after one of the midnight bandit raids. Her people called her something entirely different, but they usually spoke so rapidly—especially in the presence of foreigners—he could not make it out.

"An . . . arsenal," his smile faded as the word brought back bad memories, "will not be necessary, Raina." His eyes shifted away from hers as he scanned the dark slopes rising all around him. "Just enough ammo to get us out of the jungle . . . when we leave. Just enough to see us past any hostile rain forest occupants, such as tigers . . . or wild boars . . . though I doubt there's anything out there except tree monkeys and overgrown parrots."

Raina smiled at him knowingly, almost in defiance, but she said nothing immediately.

Ross searched the Asian faces in the distance until he found her brother's, safely in a cluster of tribesmen half his age. Clad in both loincloths and tattered fatigue pants, the forest warriors were dancing wildly to the combination of bell and drumbeats. Empty coconuts and thick gourds were lined up like primitive xylophones, filled with varying degrees of water to alter the sound they produced when struck with short sticks and stone hammers. The result was a melodic rhythm that brought the dark jungle alive, yet kept its animals strangely quiet as they watched the proceedings curiously from their branches, lairs, and caves.

Ross thought back through the chain of events that had led to this unique scene. It had begun with their last mission, where, in Saigon, a mere fifty miles to the east, they had silenced a rather outspoken critic of American involvement in Southeast Asia—the woman had just happened to be a popular rock singer and rising screen starlet, and the liberals Stateside were still in an uproar over that one.

While winding down from the hit and all the stress surrounding it, one of his men had come across an article in the *Stars & Stripes* about a beautiful Cambodian princess who was having more than her share of problems with drug-running bandits along the border region of her province.

More on a dare than anything, Ross had chased his team out of Saigon using everything from Renault taxis to three-wheeled cycles—just to see who could make it up to the Khmer border first. They really had had no idea at all how they'd go about finding the princess or her people once they got there, and the Vietnamese authorities at Go Dau Ha had nearly had them deported. But the group had persevered, and with the help of a notorious Tu Do Street cabbie had eventually made their way, via a confusing maze of jungle hamlets and valley checkpoints, to one of the princess's outlying base camps.

Circumstances had changed drastically by the time Ross and his people were granted permission to enter the isolated Svay Rieng sanctuary. No longer were the quiet, peace-seeking Khmers just struggling to endure the random harrassment raids of the Chinese bandits; the princess's brother had become a prisoner of the drug kingpin, and the bold Chinaman was demanding an outrageous ransom the Khmers would never be able to raise.

But the Khmers, adept as they were to survival in the jungle, had also never heard of deep-penetration counterinsurgent teams. And they had never seen a telescopic sniperscope.

Within forty-eight hours of their arrival, Ross's splendid little squad had proudly presented the princess with her rescued brother and the head of the gangleader.

Ross grinned as he watched his men flirting with the young maidens by the light of the flickering campfires. He would have taken out the Chinaman in *twenty-four* hours had it not been so difficult to isolate him from his goon platoon of bodyguards. The incensed horsemen were still probably galloping about the hills to the north, searching for the silent death that had reached out from the dark and snatched away their captive prize, and their leader's skull.

It was times of intense job satisfaction like these that Ross found himself musing about medals and decorations. He wished he could write Collins up a citation—the man deserved at least an ArCom for the way he'd made the Chinaman's head roll fifty feet despite the thick vegetation. But he knew old man Y back at the Penatagon wouldn't hear of it. They were a squad that didn't exist. None of their operations were on paper anywhere, or so they said. He doubted this, but he hoped so much was fact. He was confident Y would disavow any knowledge of the team's activities should they be caught red-handed in the middle of one of their missions. And that's the way it should be, he lied to himself. It added spice to the whiskey . . . and salt to the wound.

"And which young lady will you choose to share the night with, Justin Ross?" The princess leaned into his thoughts as she swayed across his field of vision. The clearing extended nearly a hundred yards beneath the enclosed canopy, with only a rare tree here and there rising between campfires, but the smoke from the celebration was collecting on its outer fringes, like blue-grey mist, lending a surrealistic haze to the activities.

Ross started to look into her softly gleaming eyes, but avoided the trap and glanced away. "Oh, I'm sure I'll just tend to my own sleeping bag tonight, Princess. Something tells me tomorrow is going to be a big day. I think all my boys oughta refrain from partaking of the jungle juice tonight. . . ." His eyes came to rest on a group of young women who had donned a dragon costume of leaves and tassels. Like a colorful Chinatown float, each girl placing her hands on the hips of the one in front of her, the group slowly danced in and out of the string of campfires, the tempo of the music growing more ominous and frantic, and—Ross was confident—the musicians becoming more intoxicated. Forgetting the princess was only a whisper away, he flexed his wrist muscles by gripping the submachine gun with both hands. *If only he were twenty years younger . . . how he'd do it all over differently. . . .*

The princess didn't miss the rippling forearms. Swallowing her sudden surge of excitement and forcing the desire from her eyes, she rose to her knees and said, "Very well, Lieutenant." Her tone was a collage of respect, despair, and disappointment. "Get your beauty sleep. I'll see to it your men are provided for accordingly. The . . . 'party' will go on until the participants exhaust themselves, but I will make sure your squad is not disturbed."

Resisting the urge to change his mind, Ross produced his best Hollywood smile and treated her to a casual salute, then said simply, "Thank you, Your Highness," in Cambodian. He bowed slowly, still sitting; frowning, she turned her back on him and walked away.

Ross started to get up, but paused when he noticed Chandler still sitting alone beside one of the campfires. He would have given a month's pay to know what was going through the man's mind. What was *really* going through the man's mind. Not the story he'd get if he went up and asked. Not the modest recital all soldiers were good at when caught reminiscing about past battlefields—be they in war or romance.

The young Cambodian woman sitting on the other side of the campfire stared through the flames, also watching Chandler closely. Waiting, as if in a game, to see what his next move would be. For surely he was up to something—some foreigner's strange brand of magic. Why else would he nurse a single flask of wine in solitude and do nothing but stare at the bright light for hours on end?

She watched the flames dancing in his eyes, and tried to find the story that was playing in his mind— for Cambodians believe that if you look into one's eyes long enough and hard enough you can sometimes read their thoughts—but all she saw were sky- blue orbs that stared back at her, unseeing and uncaring. At first, she found the game fun. He could ignore her all he wanted, and she would sit on the other side of the campfire, displaying her most sensual poses, her most innocent smiles, her most naive winks. But now the festivities were winding down, and this man was sending a shiver through her, because he was staring through the flames and past her—to a world she would never be a part of.

Chad Chandler was watching that firefight thirteen years earlier—the battle in Korea that always returned to haunt him when liquor weakened his mental defenses, allowing painful memories to weave through the punji sticks of his mind . . . to penetrate the concertina guarding his soul.

Chandler was seeing Camp Starburst in its final night of glory—after the day-long skirmishes between its defenders and the invading Chinese had culminated with the fort burning to the ground. He was watching the Communist sergeant rounding up survivors—covered with blood, they thought he was dead, and Chandler adopted quickly to the part, remaining still as stone—watching the Chinaman casually order the execution of every American still breathing.

Unable to move because of his wounds—he had been shot in both legs—Chandler finally drifted into shock. He awoke four days later in Pusan, at a mobile army surgical hospital, where they told him that, except for two men who were listed as Missing In Action, he was the only survivor of the attack. Camp Starburst had been wiped off the face of the earth, except for the ashes. And before he had awakened from his coma, the blizzard had covered even them.

The survivors? he could still remember sitting up in his bed suddenly, yelling the question at the startled nurses, pulling the tubes from his arm. Johnny, they told him. Private Johnny Pruitt. But he was MIA—nobody knew if he was dead or alive. Everyone knew that being a prisoner of the Chinese was a fate worse than death.

And the other man? What about the other man?

The lone sentry on the south perimeter, they told him. Nobody knew his name, and the camp rosters had all been destroyed in the fire. All they knew was that he was a black soldier, a quiet type—an enlisted man who had never made any waves.

A guard who had never fallen asleep on duty before. Chandler ground his teeth in thought as the flames from the campfire continued to dance in his eyes.

2.

Chandler had awakened with snakes before; this was not the first time. But in the past, he had usually been able to tell by their weight and the harshness of their scales against his nakedness whether or not they possessed venomous fangs. But this was Cambodia, and he was not confident his guess would be the right one.

So, though the end of his nightmare had almost made him sit abruptly upright in a cold sweat, Chad lay where he was, unmoving, patiently waiting for the reptile to unwrap itself from his left leg. A frightened eyelid popping open had been the only relief he afforded himself, and now, as the heavy snake slithered out from beneath his sleeping mats, he slowly scanned the camp around him.

Everything seemed as it should be. Smoke from the fires still drifted in and out of the blackened piles of wood, clinging to the floor of the rain forest. Khmers slumbered on either side of him, some peacefully, others tossing and turning, wrestling with the demons of their own dreams.

High in the mass of tangled branches overhead, a

brightly colored parrot was greeting the invisible dawn with a melodic scale of chirps and long, drawn-out whistles. The sun, which Chandler knew in this stretch of Asia would be a dull, swollen orb of orange struggling to break free of the eastern horizon, remained hidden beyond the endless wall of trees. Even in this clearing, not a single shaft of light penetrated the shifting maze of green shroud cloaking the jungle. There was only the dull glow of light that separated day from night. Much later, after thousands of rain forest inhabitants had lost their lives to predators, the sun would climb to a position overhead, and perhaps, only then, a rare shaft of gold would descend down through the thick triple canopy.

Chandler finally let the breath he was holding slowly trickle out through parched lips—the last coils of the python were unwinding from around his ankle—when a muffled groan came from below his chin, and a warm body pressed suddenly against his chest. He immediately tensed, unable to remember anything about the night before, and instead of bolting, he prayed to buddha the snake would ignore the sudden commotion and continue on its way to some distant feeding ground.

Her scent drifted up to him now, and after the python was gone and he could hear it disappearing through the reeds that hid his sleeping position, he glanced down at the swirl of long black hair beneath his chin.

Her tiny hands still clenched in sleep, the woman who had squatted across the campfire from him all night jarred his memory, and he tried desperately to recall if they had made love before he had passed out.

The mental effort only served to worsen his arriving hangover, and Chandler abandoned it, making his hands drop to her shoulders instead.

He slowly turned her away from him, laying her on her back beneath the protective covering of animal-hide mats, and in the dim light while she still slept he inspected his prize. He guessed her to be twenty at most, with years of jungle existence etched across her brow, but innocence in the narrow lines of her eyes and cheeks. Chandler's own eyes drifted down to breasts that even in sleep jutted out at him, only the nipples flat and unaroused. He shifted the covers about slightly, wishing for more light as he followed the line down her curves to where her hips widened and a dark mound beckoned him where the woman's shapely thighs came together.

The movement of the covers coaxed her from her fitful slumber, however, and suddenly she was grasping his biceps and forcing herself away from him to arms length, where she could focus on him from drowsy eyes unaccustomed to the advancing daylight.

Recognizing where she was and—he hoped—remembering him, a smile creased her lips, and she moved one tiny hand from his arm and began stroking the hair of his chest curiously.

Chandler, completely forgetting the snake now, ran his own hand down along side of her beautiful face, parting the endless swirls of hair. He lifted her chin, as if to kiss her, but she brushed it away and gently pushed him onto his back again. Then she moved her head down, resting the side of her flawless face in his lap, and began teasing him with her tongue.

Feeling himself grow immediately hard, he awkwardly arranged the covers across both of them frantically until only his face protruded out one edge, and as she engulfed him suddenly—like an animal attacking—he gasped inwardly, feeling the skin of his throat draw tight as his head drew back in ecstasy. Toes and fingers tingling as his limbs all stretched straight out to their limits, Chandler forced his tightly shut eyelids open and stared up at the vibrant leaves a hundred feet overhead, searching out the arguing birds rushing from branch to branch.

"Chad!" a husky voice intruded upon the rain forest sounds as Justin Ross's face appeared inches above his own. "How the hell are ya this morning?"

Unable to answer, Chandler just grinned back at Ross as the mats mysteriously shifted up and down a few feet away from them, the edges of his lips curling up in a demonic laugh that wouldn't come.

"Almost time for breakfast, lad!" Ross slapped him on the shoulder, ignoring the woman beneath the covers as if she were not even there.

"Yah . . ." Chandler forced the acknowledgment out in a harsh whisper as he felt his passions subside at the interruption—only to be reawakened by the woman working furiously over his crotch.

"The natives'll be up any minute," Ross continued, obviously enjoying the mental torture, "but I thought you and I would jaunt off into the woods for a little pre-breakfast jog. . . . *Come on*, Chad!" Ross cooed softly, bringing his lips closer to Chandler's ear, "Whatta ya say?"

"Sure . . . Justin . . . sure. . . ." The words came out slowly, with an utmost difficulty Ross seemed to relish. His smile brightened.

"But we won't run too far," he revealed. "Sewell tells me there's a hellacious waterfall a couple miles down that direction," he pointed to a smoky trail winding down through the looming trees behind them, "and I've arranged to have a few of the village girls here rendezvous with yours truly, for a little soapsuds scrub-down, if ya know what I mean. . . ." His eyes sparkled with latent evil, and Chandler nodded back.

"Sure . . . Justin. . . ." The mats continued to bob up and down a few feet away, seemingly more furious now, and Chad's head arced back involuntarily, his eyes closing tightly as his lips tensed. Just . . . gimme . . . some . . . time . . . to. . . ."

"To get your shit together," Ross grinned knowingly as he stood up to his full height. Towering above the helpless Chandler, he folded his arms across his chest silently, happy for the man, yet at the same time disturbed that he had found one of his troopers in the field in so defenseless a position. The irony of it—the fact that he would even bother with such worries—angered him even more. But Justin Ross just sighed as an outlet for his frustrations.

Several parrots overhead, their attention attracted to the mats mysteriously bobbing in a fashion peculiar only to wild birds, screeched their noisy protests as the action below suddenly ceased and the exhausted woman collapsed across the smiling, satiated warrior. The winged creatures' loud squawking served to cover the retreating footfalls as

Justin Ross backed away from the two lovers, embracing his own mistress as he vanished into the swirling jungle mists.

"There is no way I can persuade you to stay?" Princess Raina locked eyes with Ross as they sat amongst a hundred of her people, miles from their evening campground, atop a flat plateau that rose up through the rain forest. *"Nothing?"* Her question, soaked in anticipation, was a hushed whisper none around them could hear.

Ross thought back to earlier that morning, when at the waterfall Chandler had failed to show up. As did the maiden girls.

Only the princess had arrived.

A pleasant warmth settled over him as he relished in the memory of their encounter: She had taken his hand and led him down to the small pool of steaming water below the waterfall, and at its soft, vine-covered banks, had unfastened her modest sarong, letting it fall around her feet until she stood unclothed before him, permitting his inspection. Unsmiling, she had seemed to stare into his soul, but he had refused to play *that* game, and had instead allowed his own eyes to fall to the full breasts beneath her throat. The woman's nipples were already taut, swelling to their limits for him, craving his caress. He had allowed her to remove his own garments, as his eyes darted about the trees suspiciously, wondering how many of her bodyguards watched and judged them then and there. And though she had allowed him to move his lips against the nape of her neck as she slid his trousers off, she would not permit him to kiss her yet.

Both naked then, she had taken his arms, still facing him, backing slowly into the lagoon, spreading her legs as the water took the slight weight off her feet and set her afloat.

Lacing her fingers behind his head, the princess had pulled him in against her, until Ross too was snatched off balance by the swirling bubbles that had brought him gently to rest against her frame. Her arms and legs had suddenly wrapped around him, pulling him down on top of her, and as they'd slowly descended to the clear depths of the lagoon, he had spread her thighs apart even farther with his own and had slid powerfully into her.

Air bubbles had exploded from her lips as she gasped with the pleasure, and with the tiny silver spheres racing to the surface like balloons at a parade, he had thrust into her again and again, ignoring the warning bells of instinct screaming at him for oxygen.

Then she was smiling, her eyes still tightly closed, air bubbles escaping from the edges of her lips, and she had pushed him away; as their feet touched the bottom of the pool she had let her knees bend slightly under her weight and then had sprung toward the surface, leaving him behind.

Ross had ignored the huge multicolored angelfish darting about in front of his face and the brilliant layers of coral beneath his barefeet, and had pushed off in pursuit, quickly overtaking her before she could ascend through the twenty feet of water above.

They'd exploded above the surface amidst a spray of foam and laughter, and swimming wildly, he had chased her to the bank, where she'd surrendered meekly, rolling onto her back for him, the smile fading as she opened herself again to him. Ignoring the serious look in her dark eyes—the implications . . . the responsibilities her expression cast at him—Ross had plunged into her, forcing her tight haunches deeper into the white sand with each thrust, until the jungle fell silent all around them, and the birds in the branches overhead had stared down curiously, intrigued by the strange animal groans rising from the deeply tanned forms slapping against each other in the mist of the secret waterfall. . . .

"What?" Ross was rocked to one side slightly as Princess Raina gently punched him in the ribs in a manner none of those around them could see.

"I asked if there was no way I could convince you to stay with my people," she repeated. "What *are* you daydreaming about, Justin Ross?" Her eyes narrowed and a slight smile flashed across her features as she twisted his nipple playfully. "*Me*, I hope," she said, as her own mind flashed back briefly to their morning on the banks of the lagoon.

Ross glanced out at the tribesmen all around, their women beside them, the maidens—innocent and unclaimed—in the background, their animals beyond the outer circle. He surveyed the edges of the plateau and the beauty of the jungle rising up all around, the peaceful serenity of the unmarred wilderness that hid the deceptive power of the predators lurking within the cloak of countless trees. He stared out at the distant horizon, where the deep-blue sky merged with the multi-hued shades of rain forest green, and he watched the castlelike clouds of white and silver to his left, rising miles across the awe-inspiring panorama, and the dark, ominous storm advancing on his right, its lightning bolts arcing down into the jungle miles away as its thick curtain of grey showers rolled in along the treetops, the entire downpour visible from this distance as it moved through a distant valley—almost as if in another world entirely.

"Justin," she said, tugging on his wrist until he looked down into her eyes. "Talk to me...."

He ran the outsides of his fingers through her hair, pushing it against the contours of her face as he searched for the right words. He basked in her beauty, actually gaining inner strength from it, and let his eyes fall to the healthy body straining against the layers of tight silk wrapped around her. She was more than he could ever hope to find in a woman. And this place, this... *jungle* surrounding them ... enveloping them ... threatening, yet protecting them, was really, when he slowed everything down to think about it, his vision of success ... of ultimate happiness.

He thought back to the concrete jungles of America ... all the people, the cars, the pollution, the crime and the killing—killing for no honorable purpose—and he knew that was not what he wanted.

This was his ideal sanctuary. His fortress of solitude. His castle protecting him from "progress" and the misery and ills that came with it.

But Ross knew that it was not as simple as that: one could not be expected to disappear in the wilds that easily. One would not be *allowed* to vanish beyond the rain forest wall, joining a gentle people whose idea of life was waking with the sunrise, existing within the simple guidelines of the forest—producing nothing but love and children, craving nothing but fruit from the trees and fish from the lagoons, and retiring after an exhausting night of rice wine, bamboo dancing, and love-making once the campfires were built to protect them from the prowling cats.

Mr. Y and his boys back at the Pentagon would never allow it.

Already this hidden haven was no longer a secret. At that very moment a U.S. government plane was preparing to make a pass over the clearing. Somehow, Y had tracked Ross and his men into Cambodia, and it was time to go back to work. The fun and games were over.

"I am a soldier," he said, beginning the speech she had already heard and was tired of.

"And your duty calls to you," she muttered, turning her face away as a set of dual props broke the silence in the distance.

Ross nodded somberly as the Cessna's engines grew slowly louder.

"And when is your tour of duty up?" she asked. There was the slightest hint of sarcasm in her tone.

"I'm afraid it is a . . ." he searched for the right words, ". . . a life sentence. . . ."

Princess Raina shrugged her shoulders and frowned as the aircraft made its first pass over the clearing. "Yet you are unable . . . or *refuse* to explain what this means," she said.

Ross watched Sewell and Collins leave the edge of

the group and make their way to the northernmost point on the plateau, in preparation for setting off a wind-direction smoke flare. Both in their early thirties, each man was a study in contrasts. Collins, ex-policeman and the team's small-arms expert and sniper, was a husky specimen of medium height, with light-brown hair cropped close. Prepared as always for conflict, he looked like an angry gorilla as he bounded toward the edge of the clearing, unable to find any antagonists nearby. An ex-marine, who had spent three years racing across rooftops in Ethiopia with a crack antiterrorist squad, his hobby and all-consuming passions were pumping iron and exploding bottles of gasoline with his M-40 sniper rifle.

Sewell, tall and thin, wore his hair over the ears and parted down the middle. Always the group's pessimist, he was also their chopper pilot, having flown over twelve hundred combat missions in Korea.

As they popped their canisters, and purple smoke began drifting in over the Khmers, Ross scanned the dark faces all around, choosing to ignore the princess temporarily as he sought out the other two members of his team. He quickly saw Cory—barely eighteen now with his short stature camouflaged by a mop of hair the tropical sun had bleached nearly blond—on the opposite side of the clearing, surrounded by a harem of teen-aged girls who for all their boisterousness were probably just as virginal as the kid.

Chandler was the one who worried Ross the most. A man drifting off into the land of memories-lost was a danger signal he had been taught to spot quickly. But the trancelike periods, lasting only a few hours at the most, had begun just recently—certainly there had been no sign of his depression on the last mission—and since they were on a sort of R & R, Ross had elected not to press the matter now.

He watched two Khmer women in tight sarongs without tops race across the clearing laughing after the airplane made its second low pass, and as their lithe, athletic bodies carried them through the reeds—upturned breasts firm and hardly bouncing—their harsh almost-equatorial features reminded him of Amy, and he sighed, sorry for her.

The only woman in their group, she was a war refugee of Guatemala, with Mayan features and high cheekbones that at times made her appear more Asiatic than Latino. She had been severely wounded during their last mission and was recuperating from her multiple injuries at an American installation in Tokyo. Ross was not sure she would ever be able to rejoin them, but if he knew Amy, that would be all right with her.

Ross glanced back over at the princess—he had felt her icy orbs burning into him the entire time he had been seeking out his men. "Someday soon I will explain it all to you," he announced, forcing a dry smile.

"Someday soon . . . you will leave me," she whispered in reply. "And I fear it will be forever. . . ."

They both turned their eyes away as the airplane made its final pass. A roar of approval and scattered applause went up from the people around them as a parcel appeared as a sudden black dot against the blue sky, dropping from the belly of the plane to begin its descent the thousand-odd feet to earth.

A wave of childlike awes rose through the assemblage of Khmers as there came a loud "*pop*" overhead, and a black-and-orange parachute suddenly blossomed out above the parcel, breaking its abrupt fall.

By the time Ross and the princess had raced the short hundred yards to where the parcel landed, several dozen tribesmen were already around it. Sewell and Collins began unlatching the hasps of the breadbox-sized container.

"Wait!" Ross said, but he had spotted the tiny air holes too late—Collins had already pried the metal door open with his commando knife.

There erupted from inside the box an angry rumble, and then an enraged fireball of fur charged out, fangs and claws a blur of motion as it headed directly for Collins's face.

Screaming with surprise, the team's sniper tumbled back onto his haunches as the ferret slammed into him, biting and clawing like a Tasmanian devil freed from its cage.

"*Christ!*" Sewell jumped back as the ferocious mammal attacked, aiming for the closest flesh at hand—Collins's throat. But the ex-marine's fist drew back, and as he tumbled down toward the edge of the plateau across a narrow cliff, the blade was rammed home.

A loud squeal cut across the hot sticky air moments after the crimson spray, and then the weasel-like animal lay dead, its head severed by the sharp commando knife. After taking a few moments to catch his breath, Collins finally sat up, eyes still wide, his hands covered with blood.

The tribesmen gathering around him in a half-circle, their mouths agape in terrified silence, displayed eyes equally as wide, and they slowly drew closer to the American, frightened by all the blood, but curious as to what magic had attacked him from the sky.

"Better get something on that," Ross said, breaking the eerie quiet as he went down on one knee before Collins and motioned toward a deep gash in one of his fingers, from which blood squirted with each frantic heartbeat, like a tiny fountain.

"Damn that asshole, Y, and his practical jokes!" Collins ignored the wound and plopped the limp ferret in his lap to examine it. "Now I'll probably come down with rabies . . . or something more exotic. . . ."

Several of the Khmers moved even closer as the furry mammal was produced for their inspection. Chandler stared down at all of them from the center of the plateau; they looked like a painting from some century-old African safari: white man dazed and on his haunches, the natives gathered all around as they crowded the cliff's edge . . . a breath-taking panorama of steaming jungle and misty waterfalls spreading out beyond and below them. And for just a moment he wanted to bolt away right then and there, taking the girl who clung to his waist, forever pledged to him by their single night beneath the treetops.

Chandler knew the parcel contained something other than a rude greeting in the form of a hungry ferret. It held their next mission, and he was not in the mood for it. He was not ready for more death, more risks, more stress. More secrets no one would ever learn about, more battles they would never be able to talk about. . . .

The Cessna appeared along the edge of the tree line again, flying lower this time, and as it passed overhead, the pilot waggled his wings. *Mockingly,* Chandler thought to himself as he strained to recognize the pilot hidden behind an ace's cap and monstrous goggles. *Always mockingly. . . . We are the scum of the earth . . . the assassins. . . . We are the most important warriors left . . . yet the armchair commandos back at Disneyland East despise us . . . hate us. . . .* Chandler didn't doubt that even this early in the game that was Southeast Asia the brass in the War Room back at Puzzle Palace were plotting strategy . . . planning their demise. It would be better for them to cut and run now—before Ross's little group found itself on the wrong end of a midnight flame thrower. Vanish beyond the bamboo curtain. *Go native,* for crissake! Grab the hand of the woman at his side and disappear beneath the triple canopy, never to be seen again by another white man. Live off coconuts, mangos, crawdads . . . and pussy.

The last thought set Chandler to smiling, and though the woman at his side tugged at his arm in protest, he started down the hillside to join his fellow soldiers.

"What the hell is *this*!?" Collins jerked a small string from around the ferret's neck, and pulled the folded piece of paper from the hollow amulet attached to it.

"A friggin' love note!" Sewell slapped his knee and started laughing, but Ross moved quickly forward and snatched it.

His brows furrowed in deep concentration, he scanned the lines rapidly, then produced a dramatic frown.

"So what's up, Doc?" Cory appeared beside Chandler, youthful women protectively attached to each arm. He wrinkled his nose and upper lips in a Bugs Bunny impression.

"Yah," said Sewell, displaying the impatience they all felt. "Dispense with the suspense, honcho-san...."

Ross handed Collins the note, and turned his back on his men as he walked over to the edge of the cliff and gazed down at the rain forest spreading out beneath him.

Collins held the note out for all nearby to read.

Gentlemen soldiers of *mis*fortune:

Please pardon the unexpected surprise, but we at the big P must keep you in the field on your toes, am I not correct? I assure you the ebony animal bearing these tidings bore no disease—not that it would matter; you are all quite mad already anyway!

It was totally against established S.O.P. for you men to leave the Republic (Of Vietnam) without informing C & C of your destination and intentions. But it proved easy enough to track you down—you clowns *do* leave quite a trail after a night-long binge on *ba-muoi-ba* ... we're surprised you made it across the Khmer border unchallenged.

Had enough R & R? I hope so. You've got 48 hours to recuperate from your Rest And Relaxation vacation, then it's back to business. In the back of the ferret's cage are date, time, and frequency of the radio communication that will assign you your upcoming mission. Do us all a favor, gentlemen: decode it, and be there promptly as scheduled. The shit has hit the fan back here in The World. It's time to unleash the squad again.

A thousand pardons for this intrusion,

Y

"Where does he get off talking to us in that tone?" an insulted Sewell said, feigning intense hurt with his expression.

"Well, the man *does* issue the paychecks," Ross grumbled a few feet away.

"I just think he should be a little more mellow with his cropduster telegrams," said Collins, agreeing with the team's chopper pilot. "I mean, we *have* accomplished quite a lot in the last year or so—shit, we've been to hell and back, Justin . . . yet there's no end to this asshole's sarcasm." He waved the note in Ross's face.

"If it's compassion you want," Ross did not turn from the masterpiece spreading out in front of him to face Brent, "you're in the wrong line of work, mister. . . ."

"But it sucks, Lieutenant," the rifleman said, picking up on his squad leader's suddenly military tone. "It sucks to high heaven."

"Life in general sucks, Brent," he muttered, "but I guarantee you it's a far side better than the surprise Lady Death is guarding for you...."

Cory leaned closer to Chandler and whispered up at his ear, "That kinda talk gives me the creeps."

"Aw, just ignore them two," the ex-mercenary replied, staring down the harsh khaki blouse of one of the girls hugging MacArthur's arm. "They always get that way when the fun comes to an end and it's time to go back to work."

"You been actin' kinda eerie yourself, Big Chad," the kid said. He had debated making the statement, but it had slipped out before he could decide one way or the other. "I been watchin' you real close . . . and I almost wonder if I'd follow your ass into a firefight the way you always got that far-off look in your eyes lately...."

"Don't mean nothin'," Chandler said, slipping into his GI jargon as he moved away from the younger soldier. "No need wastin' mental energy pondering something like that, Cory The Kid . . . 'cause when the chips are down and the lead's flying, we'll all get our heads on straight...."

"Rather abruptly," MacArthur predicted.

"You got *that* right, pardner." Chandler turned to lock eyes with him for the first time as he drew farther away, joining the others at the cliff's edge. "You got that *damned straight* . . . dead center . . . right between the eyes...."

There he goes talking goofy again, MacArthur thought, shaking his head slowly from side to side in resignation, and as if fate had decided right then and there to make her unsolicited comment, a rifle's discharge sliced through the air.

The Americans instinctively slammed their bodies prone across the ground, but most of the Khmers only went into a half-crouch at best, as the smoking round impacted against an Asian jawbone.

The bullet splintered, tearing the man's lower jaw away with it, and the force of the shot flung the rest of his body over the cliff. His scream inhuman because of the gaping hole where his smile had once been, the Cambodian flailed his arms and legs helplessly as he plummeted hundreds of feet to the jagged treetops below.

"My Lord!" Princess Raina watched the body flop about across the green carpet and disappear into the hungry jaws of the jungle. She reached out for Justin, but he was already on his feet, running uphill across the plateau, sprinting for the tree line.

Submachine guns off their shoulders and against their hips—the slings flapping about wildly as they ran—Ross's men joined in the charge behind him.

It was doubtful any of them knew who they were up against.

Sporadic muzzle flashes greeted their zigzag advance through the clearing, and Ross answered with a volley of his own tracer rounds, sending several branches toppling and leaving two of their assailants face down in the rotting leaves of the rain forest floor.

"Move it!" Ross signaled Chandler and MacArthur to the left with his hands, and Collins and Sewell in the other direction. "And I want some prisoners, you hear me!?" He let loose another half-magazine of hot lead without aiming. Another gunman beyond the tree line screamed his life away before dropping his weapon for the last time. "I want prisoners!"

Chandler and MacArthur exchanged quizzical glances, nodded in resignation, then sent short spaced bursts of automatic fire in the general direction from which the first shots had come.

A gratifying rush of blood flowed through his veins when the army lieutenant glanced back and saw Princess Raina rallying several of her tribesmen to assist the foreigners. It was a tingling sensation of both inspiration and encouragement that ran up and down his spine and urged him forward, into the rain of hostile lead, even as his gut instincts told him to turn back. *Why die for these people?*

But the men who had ambushed them from the tree line had been shooting at Ross and his men also—the bullets were not discriminating!

"They're retreating through the trees!" Chandler called out in Spanish—an old trick they had taught each other at their training grounds back at LZ London—and Ross changed course abruptly with the new information, heading to his left, almost across the clearing now, until he could hear the snipers crashing through the dry branches and saplings that formed tangled nets between the taller trees.

"How many?" Ross called out, also in Spanish; something told him Big Chad would have the answer, though he had no idea where the ex-merc was or where he had entered the tree line.

"Four left standing!" Chandler called out from behind a wall of vines several dozen yards away. An intense spray of M-60 rounds answered him, directed at the sound of his voice.

A muffled scream pierced the jungle mists still clinging to the clearing's edge, and Ross heard a body topple into some bushes on its way down. "I'm hit!" He recognized young Cory's startled voice. "The bastards got me, Justin!" he called out frantically in English. "I'm hit!"

Another spray of automatic weapons fire, mixed with drug-induced laughter, lashed out at the Americans, and Ross could envision his men halting their charge and taking cover behind the nearest trunks.

"You still want prisoners?" he heard Sewell call out during a lull in the constant string of discharges.

Ross pulled a small fragmentation grenade from his thigh pocket and clutched the safety pin. Visions of MacArthur—still legally too young to drink with them in most bars across the globe—sprawled across the jungle floor, his lifeblood oozing from a dozen holes, flashed in front of Ross's mind's eye. No, he would have to abandon the hope of taking any prisoners.

"Fire in the hole!" he warned in Spanish, announcing his intention of throwing a grenade through the trees. But before Ross could let fly the frag, a thunderclap of explosions rolled out from within the rain forest, knocking the Americans from their feet, and disintegrating several of the men who had just tried to kill them.

3.

Ross wanted to shift his jaw about and shake the pain away, but he knew that would only make matters worse. He was still prone against the earth, the left side of his face across a mat of rotting leaves. Termites danced in front of his eyes as gunsmoke drifted before his nostrils. A noisy lizard slithered beneath his boots and ran on its hind legs from the clearing, hissing angrily as it disappeared into the trees from which the explosion had just emanated. Secondary blasts were still erupting beyond the tangle of vines, and another tree trunk fell against the earth with a jarring thud, only a few feet from his head.

In the distance, Cory MacArthur could be heard groaning softly in muted agony, a rustling in the leaves evidence some of his friends had rushed to his side.

Ross concentrated first on the immediate kill zone radiating out around him: he could detect no one approaching... could not *feel* any enemies nearby—a soldier's craft that took years of experience in the bush, honing that gut-instinct edge. Then he slowly replaced the safety pin in the grenade and slipped it into a carrier pouch on his belt. He moved his other arm, then his leg. Everything appeared to be in working order. He let out a heavy sigh of relief—something he never would have done fifteen years earlier, as a green recruit . . . on his first battlefield.

A short, five-round burst from an American-made submachine gun broke the hushed silence that had settled over this misty stretch of rain forest, and soon Chandler was calling out at the top of his lungs, "Checkered flag, grunts! End of contest. . . ."

Ross pushed himself up into a wobbly crouch, then rose to his feet and forced himself to run through the maze of wild hedges in the direction of his demo man's voice.

"One there," Chandler pointed out a body, face down a few feet away, "and two on the other side of that tree stump," he motioned to three boots sticking up out of the piles of leaves behind them.

"What's this?" Ross bent down and picked up a severed arm. The jungle floor, rich in crawling pests, had already dispatched a squad of gnats to attack the bloodied limb, and as Ross held it out at arm's length to keep the shredded ligaments from soiling his clothes, several bugs fluttered away on humming wings.

Chandler didn't immediately answer the lieutenant. Instead, he walked over to a nearby tree, and producing his calf knife dug a sliver of shrapnel from the bark. Wiping off the sap that had "bled" from the tamarind's wound, he said, "One of us is better than just a damned-good sharpshooter. I'd say a tracer or two slammed into that poor bastard's backpack," he pointed down to the Asian whose skull he had just splattered across the jungle floor moments ago, "which was either filled with frags or RPGs...."

Sewell ran up beside them just then, right hand tensed on his machine gun. He was breathing hard, and was not yet convinced the firefight was over. He glanced around warily, paying little attention to the bodies littering the battleground, searching instead for potential combatants still lurking somewhere in the trees. His expression told them he was on the verge of saying something, but he swallowed hard instead, choking slightly, and Ross resumed examining the sliver of metal Chandler had handed him.

"I'd say it's ChiCom," he decided, turning the warm chunk over and over in the palm of his hand, "but not a frag—more like a shoulder-launched projectile...."

Chandler glanced around at the thriving flora already clinging to his feet, searching for the telltale fiberglass tubes he knew he'd never find.

"Christ!" Sewell nearly stumbled over a severed leg as he walked over to one of the bodies for a closer look. He reached down, grabbed the corpse's shoulder, and turned the decapitated body over onto its back.

"Wait!" Ross yelled, visions of a crafty Communist private having the last laugh by clutching a grenade beneath his belly—to be activated only after he was turned over by his pursuers or scavengers.

But this particular soldier had had no time to put into play such an elaborate booby trap. The motion set his gun arm rigid and into action, however; a full magazine of copper-jacketed rounds, mixed with green tracers, erupted inches from Sewell's face, spouting forth like a noisy, colorful fountain on the Fourth of July. The sizzling tracers arced up into the trees, piercing the triple canopy of branches which grew together high overhead. Leaves fluttered down by the hundreds, and terrified monkeys scampered over one another in their haste to escape, hundreds of feet aboveground. Mouth agape, Sewell fell back onto his buttocks, speechless. "*Jesus* Christ!" he screamed, reaching beneath him and producing another bloodied limb—this time an arm, its gnarled brown fingers fully extended.

Chandler glanced up at the leaves still descending from the green ceiling above, grinned after he became satisfied the last of the branches had fallen, then rushed over to Sewell and clasped the dead fingers in a hearty handshake and began pumping the lifeless limb. "Glad to meet ya, Jesus!" he laughed, causing Ross to shake his head from side to side in resignation. "Mighty proud to meet ya!"

"The gods have nothing to do with this," a feminine voice behind them announced softly, and the Americans turned to find Princess Raina, between two of her lumbering bodyguards, standing at the edge of the tree line, mist and gunsmoke swirling about their legs.

"They not Communist," the man on her left declared, motioning toward the bodies. "They loot . . ." he searched his mind for the appropriate words in English. "They thieve. . . ."

"Bandits," the princess expounded. "Scum from the same group who kidnaped my brother."

"Pretty heavy artillery for civilian free-lancers."

Ross lifted an AK from beside one of the dead men, and an American-made M-60 from under another.

"They returned for vengeance," she said. "I presume they meant to kill you round-eyes." There was no smile on her face despite the choice of words. "The method in which you killed their leader left them with much loss of face. They sensed you were leaving. They would never be able to live with the humiliation after you left . . . once they would have to share the jungle with us again. I fear we have not seen the last of them. . . ."

"We in store for bookoo grief," the bodyguard's pidgin English set Chandler to dancing around one of the corpses. Still shaking the dismembered hand, blood flying about in a crimson spray, he began chanting: *"Yea!* Though I dance through the valley of the shadow of death, I will fear no evil—*do you hear me, you cocksuckers hiding out there in the trees?*—For I am the meanest motherfucker in the whole damned valley!"

Startled by all the sudden profanity, Princess Raina's eyes fell to the ground while her bodyguards left her side and began examining the bodies for valuables.

"What about Cory?" Ross leaned forward as he closed in on the team's medic, Sewell. "Why the hell did you leave him, Matt?"

The thin chopper pilot shook the shocked expression off his face and closed his mouth. Taking several seconds to blink himself back to reality, he finally said, "The kid's okay, Justin. All he took was a flesh wound." Sewell wiped the beads of sweat from his forehead, then, using his fingers, combed his dark hair straight back. "And a sliver of shrapnel that—"

"What?" Ross leaned forward closer this time, until the two men were nose to nose.

"Went clean through!" Sewell was quick to explain. "Mighta dinged a nerve in his leg, to tell you the truth—that's what all the crying was about—but he'll be okay, Lieutenant . . . trust me. . . ."

Ross frowned at the request, his mind flashing back to the army recruiter he had met a lifetime ago. "But will he be any good to me in the upcoming mission? Am I gonna have to med-evac his ass out?"

"Naw . . . naw," Sewell scooted back a few inches, then staggered to his feet and began brushing himself off. "Collins is back there with him holding a bandage in place—I showed him how to elevate and apply direct pressure, which I guess he already knew anyhow—"

"Get to the point, Matt!" Ross's eyes narrowed. "Have we got a casualty or haven't we?"

"Fuck me if I misjudge this one, Lieutenant. A night in the rack with some of these Orientals-of-questionable-virtue walking back and forth across his buttocks, and the kid'll be good as new."

"Fine." Ross turned Sewell politely around. "Now get your own butt back there and make sure Brent don't put a tourniquet around Cory's neck or something!"

"I'm gone, Justin!" Sewell vanished between two towers of clinging vines. "I'm history, bwana-san. . . . Dust on the wind!"

Ross didn't bother himself listening for further grumblings from the team liberal. He quietly clapped debris off his hands as though he had just spent a day in some suburban garden, then turned to face Princess Raina.

"Looks like you might be needing our services for a little while longer," he said.

"But you are a soldier," she replied, beginning to mock him. "And your duty and your destiny—"

"Our actions brought this grief down on your people," he cut her off, not in the mood for word games. The jungle was already a too-complex *mind* game. "If we hadn't ambushed those Chinamen in the manner we did—"

"It was necessary to secure the release of my brother," she interrupted; he again cut her off, waving a hand to silence her.

"If we hadn't chosen to liberate their gangleader's head from the rest of his body with a hot round, perhaps they wouldn't have taken the whole matter so personally," he smiled for the first time.

Princess Raina giggled slightly, and her hand shot up to cover her mouth in the habit peculiar to many Asian women. "Yes," she agreed, eyes softening finally. "Your skillful trick with the tracer definitely left an impression on Lu-long's followers. We forest dwellers believe that one who has been beheaded at death is forever forced by the spirits to wander the place where they died—unable to find heaven or hell. . . ."

"It appears to be quite a widespread belief," Ross nodded, thinking back to the Communist insurgent who had lost his skull to one of Collins's sniper bullets back in Bangkok, and to *all* the men who had lost their heads because of his team's activities across the face of Vietnam.

"Of that I'm sure...." the princess responded softly.

Ross checked the date on his Rolex, then glanced up at the branches tangled together ten stories above them. A single shaft of sunlight pierced the triple canopy, sending a dim lance down through the dust and mist and gunsmoke still drifting along on the jungle's floor. "We've two nights before we have to acknowledge our next mission, Your Highness," he bowed slightly, enjoying the irritation it brought her. "I've no idea if my ... *duty* ... will take me to Singapore or South Africa. But, until I find out, we are at your service...."

"My service?" she cocked an eyebrow up at him quizzically.

"I'd wager that within the next forty-eight hours, my team can scatter those nasty opium smugglers in a fashion guaranteeing they'll never bother your people again...."

"My kingdom is this rain forest," she said, raising her arms to encompass the trees surrounding them like protective guardians. "I have no castle on the mountaintop, Justin ... no treasure chests of gold and diamonds to award you.... How do we repay foreigners like you for risking your lives in a matter which does not concern you?"

Ross glanced around; they were alone now, except for the dead men at their feet. A grin came to his lips, and he gently laid his weapon against the nearest sapling, sinking to his knees in front of her.

"Justin?" his name escaped her as he slowly wrapped his arms around her thighs and lifted her off the ground a few inches. The princess ran her fingers through Ross's hair, then laced them together behind the base of his skull. Eyes tightly shut now, her own head dropped slowly back, the skin along her throat taut and smooth as the American military officer placed his lips against the thin fabric guarding her groin. Expertly applying pressure, with both his arms and his mouth, Ross elicited a deep sigh from the woman, which drifted along on the gunsmoke and faded against the brittle sound of chirping parakeets and singing magpies.

"What's the verdict?" Chandler pulled the skewer laced with tiny fishes from the campfire and chanced a bite, then replaced the bamboo shaft over the flames, electing to cook them a little longer.

Sewell, his feet over the edge of the dried lavabed and dangling in the waters of the lagoon, gave a noncommittal expression but still sounded enthusiastic as he applied a clean bandage to MacArthur's two wounds. "No sweat, GI . . . prognosis bookoo numba one! This kid'll be kickin' ass with the rest of us, rikky-tik, no doubt about it. . . ."

Cory, his head cushioned in the lap of a sarong-clad girl sitting cross-legged beside Sewell, was smiling and eating green seedless grapes while a second Khmer maiden fanned him from behind with a large palm frond. "No, no, no. . . ." he shook his head vigorously in the negative. "Got me my million dollar wound, boys! Cory baby's not gonna participate in no more—"

"In no more *what?*" Ross's head emerged from the calm waters of the lagoon, his thin hair short and flat against his scalp. His bullet-grey eyes locked onto MacArthur's as he braced his elbows up on the stone banks. Behind him, Princess Raina broke the surface, setting dual ripples out around them. In the background, topless women in wet sarongs frolicked on the white sands of the opposite beach. Cory broke the staring contest and concentrated on the dozen bouncing breasts fifty yards away, but he felt strangely little arousal.

"Cory baby's not gonna participate in no more *what?*" Ross repeated the question.

Keeping his eyes on the women playing keep-away with a large octopus, MacArthur said, "No more behind-the-lines, seek-out-and-destroy, bordering-on-the-bizarre, secret—"

A massive hand came around the youth from behind and clamped itself across Cory's mouth. After silencing him, Chandler, who had appeared from within the tree line bordering the lagoon's edge, sat down beside MacArthur, a brotherly smile on his lips, but a serious cast to his eyes. "Granted, this ain't no bar, boy . . . and we ain't drunk on tainted '33, but these here ladies of the lust muscle," Big Chad motioned to the girls making Cory comfortable, "are about as bi-fucking-lingual as a Cambodian can get," he said, pausing to wink at one of the frowning maidens. "So watch your mouth, son . . . or I'll have to do us all a favor and break your goddamned jaw, okay?"

But Cory was not one to be easily intimidated, even incapacitated as he was. "I'm just sick and tired of all the military bullshit, Chad," he whined for Ross's benefit. "Why risk our skin for the Green Machine—

who don't give a damn about us anyway—when we can just lay back here in this jewel of a jungle and *relax* the rest of our lives?" The kid posed the question innocently, and Chandler glanced over at Ross. Both veterans exchanged knowing looks, and—like those rare moments on the battlefield—Chandler felt he could read the lieutenant's mind: they were all getting tired of the sport. The hunt. Especially the times when they became the hunted.

And after all the wild rain forests they had struggled through, grasping at the strings of life while the current of death dragged them through the cesspools of the Far East, here finally was a stretch of peaceful jungle where even the tigers left you alone. Where you could hang up your holster and lounge on the beach the rest of your life, lying beneath a bare-breasted virgin with grapes dangling from her fingers. Where the Commies and their grand revolution had yet to hear of. Where a plane crash could be faked and even the Special Forces would go away convinced none of them had survived. *Not even charred molars, General: that's the last of them damn war dogs!*

Ross felt the mental contact between himself and the big ex-mercenary. It both mystified and worried him, and he broke it off, ever-aware he was the squad leader, and that it just wouldn't do to go fantasizing about retiring to a Khmer commune. Directing one last disapproving glare at MacArthur, he turned to face Princess Raina, then slowly let his head submerge beneath the surface of the water until he had licked her nipples erect again.

Allowing him the customary few seconds for his

pleasure—and hers—she pushed away, giggling like a schoolgirl, and floated on her back to the center of the lagoon.

His own back still to his men, Ross tired of her, and bracing his elbows atop the harsh volcanic stone that formed one bank of the lagoon, pulled himself up out of the water. He was totally naked, but no one seemed to notice, and instead of covering himself with a towel or robe, he just sat there, basking in a rare ray of sunlight that filtered down through the trees, his arms locked behind, supporting him. "Time to get back to business," he said, forcing the words out as he felt the heat from the Asian sun quickly dry his skin and begin its attempt at burning him. Squinting, he stared up at it—because of the heavy mists from the waterfall and the triple canopy he could do that without endangering his vision—and, as expected, the orb was flat and orange, not small and blinding white. That meant it would soon be sunset: never mind its apparent angle in the sky. Terrain in the jungle was deceptive. The hills and the peaks, the trees and the mists played games on the mind.

It *would* soon be sunset.

"I'm sooooo tired of shop talk," Cory lamented, sighing heartily—again for Ross's benefit, but the lieutenant ignored the teenager.

"Princess Raina will supply us with some guides after nightfall. At this very moment, runners are pinpointing the exact location of the gang of drugrunners that has been tormenting her splendid little kingdom here.

"Well, tonight we hit 'em where it hurts. We hit

'em with everything we've got. And we hit 'em hard."

"I love that kind of talk, Roscoe," Collins, the sniper, said, producing his most shit-eating grin as he cracked some knuckles for emphasis. "Yes sir, I love it more than an obscene phone call!"

"Oh brother." Sewell rose to his feet and abandoned his T-shirt before diving into the lagoon with his jeans on. Ross watched him swim to the bottom of the pool, directly beneath Princess Raina—he knew what the ace chopper pilot was setting his sights on. But he didn't really care. Instead, he glanced down at the T-shirt lying across the crag of black lava. Across the front was stenciled: Gimme Head Till I'm Dead.

Ross did not smile, though the five words were the funniest phrase he had seen since leaving the massage parlors of Tu Do Street. He wanted to cross his fingers for luck, though he knew he was already too prone to being superstitious. He just hoped the T-shirt was not an omen . . . that Matt Sewell would be able to engage in fellatio for many years to come.

I'm getting powerful-bad vibes about this, Chad Chandler thought to himself as he reached the halfway point up the rope.

Princess Raina's runners had returned to tell them the Chinese opium gang had set up camp in a new hideout: limestone caves located midway up a sheer cliff face that was accessable only by bamboo ladders which were withdrawn after dark.

The cliff itself rose from the jungle floor several hundred feet, piercing the triple canopy in several places, and the caves were some five to six stories off the ground.

They had reconned the area shortly after sunset, learning that only two sentries were left at the base of the cliff after the ladders were pulled up. One man was posted at the lip of the middle cave—there were three small openings the size of a human, separated by ten to twenty feet—and smoky campfires were visible just inside each limestone mouth, boisterous and intoxicated figures dancing and fighting behind the flickering flames. A collage of confusing shadows, twice the size of the men creating them, also danced about on the walls inside the caves—making it difficult for Ross to judge the number of renegades left in the gang.

At first, Ross had planned on simply sending a LAW rocket or M-79 thumper round into the midst of the Chinese, killing them all with one carefully placed shot. But after learning of the cliff-and-caves scenario, he had decided an assault on the difficult position would help tone his team for whatever was to come ... whatever was waiting for them in Saigon.

Chandler glanced up: there was still no activity on the outer lip of the middle cave opening.

After taking out the sentries on the ground, (it had been easy enough; he and Collins had simply crawled up behind the sleepy guards and pulled them up off their feet with garrote wires wrapped firmly around their throats until their boots ceased kicking ... except for the spasms), Ross had thrown a three-pronged grappling hook the Khmers had fashioned from bamboo up onto a sturdy tree trunk that jutted out from the face of the cliff, and on the first attempt, had managed to secure it.

Running a few feet above the trunk was a narrow ledge where the ladders were stored. Beyond this precipice, which hung fifty feet out over the jungle floor, began the shallow footholds that led the rest of the way up to the caves. Ross's major worry was that they might be booby-trapped, but the lack of discipline among the sentries on the ground had only served to reinforce his suspicions that the gang members possessed little military skill or survival cunning, but were instead simple hoodlums, with more amateurs than professionals in their ranks, and no organization.

The lead man in the assault team, Chandler was glad the canopy of branches overhead blocked out the stars and moonlight—if there *was* any up there. The flickering campfires were crackling with hot embers that sent glowing ash fluttering down along the cliff face, and when he glanced below him once, Chandler was startled to see the light from the campfires reflected in the dual pools of blood that had collected next to the camouflaged bodies of the sentries. Don't look back, he told himself. Never look down. . . . And he commanded his right hand over his left, and continued slowly up the rope.

Sewell and Collins were directly under him, submachine guns and thirty pounds each of explosives slung over their shoulders. Ross was seventy yards across from the cliff wall, on the other side of the clearing. He had elected to try his hand at Brent's sniper rifle; it would be his job to take out any Chinese unfortunate enough to venture over to the edge of the cave entrance for a gander at the ground. Reluctantly, the enlisted men had all agreed that termination by rifle discharge would not apply to drunkards simply relieving themselves over the lip of the ledge.

But the mouths of all three caves were deserted when Chandler reached the top of the rope and began the swift and silent climb up the face of the cliff, using only the footholds carved into the limestone.

Though the men behind him made no noise either, Chandler knew they were only a few feet away—in a strange sort of way, he could "feel" their confidence radiating out ahead of the group as their shadowy forms cut through the thick, humid air on their way to conflict and carnage.

This was the way Big Chad liked it: when he was among the aggressors . . . the ambush team who chose the time, place, and method of attack . . . the men who delivered, unannounced, the death blow from the dark.

As he grew nearer the last foothold, Chandler's mind—unbelievable as it seemed—began to wander, and he flashed back to that incident in his youth, when he had been working at an all-night convenience store. . . .

The place had been located across from a vast, murky lake, where—neighborhood legend had it—a woman had murdered her two children years earlier, chopped them up into little pieces, and scattered their remains across the moonlit ripples before taking her own life by drowning. There had always been a vacancy on the graveyard shift at the store; it was hard to keep good employees around when the pinball machines kicked on by themselves, or the lights went out without warning, or the front door opened and closed—with nobody around and the weather outside calm . . . not the slightest hint of wind or even a midnight breeze.

Big Chad had never put any stock in these ghost stories, of course. Even when just a high school sophomore, he had been a formidable sight in his DEATH FROM ABOVE paratrooper T-shirt his uncle in Europe had sent him. It had been his dream to reach the age of seventeen—never mind if he graduated from high school—so he could enlist in the military. A great adventure waited for him on the other side of the world—he could feel it in his soul. Nonsense about goblins and warlocks (and his buddies sneaking down to the lake when he was on duty so they could wail and scream right at the stroke of midnight was not the young man's idea of job satisfaction *or* excitement).

Even after small items like the stock pricer or his keys, or the skin magazine he had just been drooling over, had begun disappearing—only to reappear in a part of the store where he hadn't even been to that evening—Chandler hadn't become worried . . . or spooked. Despite his youth and inexperience, he had known the mind was a powerful force which, especially after lack of sleep, could play the weirdest tricks on you. (Maybe he *had* been over on that side of the shop earlier after all. . . .)

The most terrifying incident of his life to that point had occurred five weeks after he had felt he'd mastered the workings and intricacies of the graveyard shift—and it had had nothing to do with the supernatural.

Exhausted from classes in the day, work at night, and only a few hours of sleep in the evening, Chandler had been staring at the wallclock one pre-dawn morning, listening to the coffee pot gurgling like the TV commercials, totally convinced the Lady-In-The-Lake spirit was turning the hands of the clock back when he wasn't looking (the minutes sure seemed to be *dragging* by!), when the front doors had quietly blown open, a cool breeze swirling through the shop. Now such an event was not something Big Chad would get overly concerned about. He had refused to believe in the legend of the lake spirits, but he would admit to his friends that strange goings-on had occurred at the store on a routine basis—things he could not explain, but things that weren't about to scare him out of the much-needed job. To his closest friend—a junior he had spent many a summer with rafting the river wilds outside town—he had even confided about one night when someone had touched him on the shoulder from behind, and when he'd whirled around there was nobody there. Always tired from lack of sleep, he had dismissed the incident as only his imagination, and had joked he had even come to be on a one-to-one talking basis with the invisible Lady-In-The-Lake, who drifted in with the Friday night mist to have coffee with him.

So when the front doors to the store blew open during that early-morning hour, Chandler had been slow in turning to check on the distraction.

And the next thing he'd known, two very-much-alive hoodlums had been upon him from behind, slamming pistol butts against his head as they wrestled him to the door.

Overpowered and stunned, Chandler had lain with his face against the cool concrete floor as they continued to beat him. More punks rushed into the store as the men above kicked him in the sides repeatedly, and they'd overturned several displays and smashed a huge glass case containing cheap costume jewelry and novelties from some Indian reservation.

At first, he hadn't been able to understand what was going on. True, the store had been robbed in the past—but that was years ago, and after a recent crackdown on area gangs by the police, the neighborhood had quieted down considerably. The first thought that had come to his mind was that some enemy from his past had chosen this particulat night to wreak havoc and revenge on him and his store. But even as they'd slammed him into the concrete and rifled the cash register, he hadn't been able to recall anyone he had wronged during his life who could possibly harbor this much anger and resentment.

"This is a holdup, you dumb shit!" one of them had finally announced, after they had pulled out a handful of his hair and broken his nose. "We want the combination to the safe!"

A flood of relief had washed through him after it had become clear what was going on. At least it was nothing personal. At least—

But it *was* personal!

They had snuck up on him in the dead of night—and that was embarrassing. They had attacked him from behind—and that was dirty pool. And then they had been about to splatter his brains across the cold cement floor—and the thought of giving his life for such a worthless cause . . . the thought of dying before he could enlist in the military and venture to some distant battlefield overseas to kill or be killed *honorably* had been more than he could bear!

Though the man with a knee in his back had also held a pistol to the base of his skull and had been repeatedly threatening to pull the trigger, Chandler had felt no fear. Only desperation: he *had* to survive the confrontation. He would *not* give up his life so easily . . . without a fight.

And somehow he had been able to tell . . . to *feel* . . . the maniac leaning over him hadn't given a damn about the money either—he had only wanted to murder somebody that night. He had only wanted to feel the power of death against his trigger finger . . . taste blood on his lips. It hadn't mattered that there was no sport in the "kill"—that the victim wouldn't have been allowed even a slight quotient survival. It had been plain to every man in the room that the gunman only wanted to see someone or something squirm before it died.

The thing that had made young Chad Chandler grit his teeth as they pressed his face against the concrete floor was his own carelessness: had he not been daydreaming when they'd entered the store, he might have been able to grab the revolver under the counter . . . might have at least brought some smoke down on the bastards before they filled him full of holes, but it had appeared he would die like a dog with its tail between its legs.

The moment he resisted, they'd have cracked his skull in two with a cylinder full of hot loads. And if he'd passively submitted, the same thing would have happened.

Chandler had tensed his leg muscles, preparing to flip over and die staring into the eyes of the coward at his back, when the plate glass windows at the front of the store had exploded and two of the hoods had flown back off their feet—catapulted away from the front doors by a storm of pellets from four police riot shotguns.

Before Chandler had been able to react, the gunman above him had lost his chest to a secondary wave of buckshot, and as pistols clattered to the floor on either side of him and bodies toppled over his own, the kid had felt a new fear: would the officers mistakenly shoot him, too?

There had been a flurry of activity around him as spit-shined shoes went from body to body, kicking weapons away, and then he had been roughly turned over onto his back and searched as an attack dog stood poised inches from his face, snarling loudly and anxious to pounce.

But its handler had refused to give the desired command, and when Chandler opened his eyes, he had been staring up at a smiling watch commander—a stocky old sergeant with a year left until retirement.

"I work here! I work here!" he'd yelled, as the police dog bolted closer, only to be restrained at the last moment by its thick leather leash. "I'm the victim! I'm the fucking victim!"

And, though several of the officers had kept long-barreled revolvers casually trained on him, the patrol sergeant had nodded his head in a friendly manner and, still smiling, said, "We know, son... we know.... Been watchin' these scumbags for weeks now. Knew they were gonna hit one of these joints... just didn't know where the post-mortem would eventually go down...."

"You're lucky to be alive," another patrolman had said producing an ear-to-ear grin as several ambulances had started rolling up to the scene.

"Count your blessings, my friend." A corporal with scars crisscrossing his chin had stared completely through him as he helped Chad to his feet. "These low-life punks gunned down a gas station attendant five years ago...."

"Out on parole already," the sergeant had remarked, shaking his head bitterly.

"Fucking courts," muttered the corporal.

"You're lucky to be alive," the patrolman had repeated somberly.

And Chad had naively nodded his head in agreement, relief suddenly flooding through him as he watched the ambulance attendants draping sheets over the faces of three of the gunmen.

As officers led two of the suspects out to the patrol cars in handcuffs, Chandler had watched the hoods saunter away, cool and calm, their backs to him—one giggling at all the gunplay... how this would only serve to bolster his jailhouse reputation. The other had glanced over his shoulder back at Chandler as he went through the shattered doorway. He had locked eyes with the high school student and had given a knowing nod—one which Chandler hadn't been able to interpret.

Did it signify an unspoken understanding between

criminal and victim... that there was nothing personal in all this... that they were both survivors, and, therefore shared something almost sacred? Or was the nod merely the defiance, and a warning young Chad hadn't survived at all, but was only living on borrowed time.

Chad hadn't spent much time pondering the encounter, searching for hidden meanings. But he had allowed himself a week to reflect on the incident and its aftermath.

Chad Chandler had submitted his resignation.

Minimum wages just didn't justify sacrificing his life for store property. He had never been a company man anyway. And during that month of the twilight of his youth, the kid had promised himself two things: that he would learn the arts of death and destruction better than any punk on the block, and that, never again, would he allow man or beast to sneak up on him like that. Never again would he become a victim. Never again would he feel cool concrete against the side of his face, or the helplessness that came when a coward armed with a firearm pressed the pistol to the back of your head and told you to kiss your ass good-bye....

All these memories raced before Chandler's mind's eye as he advanced on the entrance to the middle cave of the limestone cliff.

At first he was not sure why the flashbacks had flooded over him at this particular moment, but then, as he grew nearer potential conflict with the Chinese in the cave, he realized the reason: if he encountered any dozing sentries inside the mouth of the cave entrance, he would be seizing the advantage just like the gunmen in the convenience store had nearly two decades earlier. He would be unleashing a surprise attack more violent than the one that had been mounted against him.

The only difference was these victims would never feel the helplessness Chandler had felt when the men had robbed his store and held his face against the floor for what seemed like ages. These victims would not endure mental torture, like the kind that had been inflicted on him by a paroled madman. These victims would not soak their pants with urine or be saved at the last moment by tall heroes with sparkling badges.

For Chad Chandler was a professional killer now, calculating his every move long before he made it. And for the bandits dancing beside campfires in the cave, death would be swift and certain.

4.

"Roscoe better be able to differentiate between the good guys with the round eyes, and—" Collins had moved up behind Chandler as they prepared to assault the caves, but his offhand remark was cut short by a spray of tracers from a high treetop on the other side of the clearing.

Sparks, puffs of white dust, and slivers of lead bounced in all around them.

"What the—" Sewell began cursing, but his words were lost in the staccato bark of several machine guns from just inside the mouth of the most distant cave.

Chandler, using a strong, underhanded movement, tossed a grenade from his web-belt pouch into the closest cavern, then quickly joined his team members as they flattened out along the narrow ledge running against the face of the cliff.

"What a cluster-fuck!" he heard Sewell still complaining as they frantically searched for crevices in which to sink, snakelike.

"What the hell went wrong?" Collins was swearing now, too, and when the grenade finally detonated, pieces of equipment and bodies rolled out the openings in the cliff wall. Screams of the wounded mingled with the sound of discharges and ricochets, and Chandler lifted his machine gun a few inches up above the closest foothold and fired a long burst of slugs in the direction of the voices.

Below, Ross was sending single shots up into the leaning tree across from his men, and soon the guerilla nestled among the fronds, who had been acting as nighttime lookout, was knocked backward through space as if he had been slammed in the belly with a baseball bat. Before he could even scream, his body flattened out across the ground with a sickening thud. His rifle bounced across the rotting jungle floor, but it did not go off.

"I'd say the bad guys got our ass pinned down!" Sewell yelled a few inches over to Big Chad, as the cave mouth filled with additional riflemen. The space around the Americans quickly became saturated with flying lead. "Anybody got any bright ideas?"

"I told you we shoulda brought MacArthur along!" Collins complained as he pulled a frag from his own belt, withdrew the pin, then heaved it at the cave entrance with the most muzzles flashing against the dark. Cory, by permission of Lieutenant Ross, had remained behind at the base camp—despite his protests—so that his healing period would not be interrupted by unnecessary antics in the field.

The grenade struck the charred limestone between the middle and most distant opening and bounced off the cliff wall. Landing a few feet away from the sniper Ross had popped out of the tree, the frag detonated with a blinding flash that propelled the corpse over onto its stomach.

"Nice shot!" Sewell quipped sarcastically, amazed with himself at being able to even open his mouth with all the lead zinging in amongst them. "How'd you ever pass the grenade course in boot camp?"

"We coulda stuck *Cory* up in one of them trees!" Collins ignored the frowning chopper pilot. "He could be zappin' those clowns right now, staring right down their throats from above, knockin' 'em over like in a lousy shooting gallery. But, no—instead we got Roscoe down on the ground playing around with my Redfield . . . in a position where he can't hit diddly-squat unless they tiptoe right out onto the edge of their—"

"Where he can't hit *what?*" Sewell cut him short as he rolled carefully over onto his back, heaving a CS canister at the nearest opening in the same movement.

The tear-gas grenade ricocheted off the wall of the entrance and bounced in, but just as it began to spew clouds of irritant, one of the Chinamen grabbed it and threw it out. "Lucky toss!" Chandler added, as the canister spiraled down to the jungle floor, bouncing loudly as it popped and crackled. It rolled up against the dead sharpshooter and stopped.

Moments later, enveloped by a ground-clinging layer of the silver gas, the bandit's clothes burst into flames. Chandler spotted the ghastly scene but said nothing—the sight would have set Collins to applauding loudly and they didn't need the attention.

A grating roar sliced through the night air just then, and a small green flare burst beside the cliff wall, a few yards above the three openings. Launched at a steeper trajectory, it would have burrowed into the canopy of interlacing branches overhead and set off a raging fire, but now it just drifted along on its parachute, bobbing from side to side, throwing a dim, flickering light across the scene of battle.

All three Americans turned to look over their shoulders to see who had launched the projectile—they knew Ross wasn't carrying any—but the men in the caves had set up a nest of heavy machine guns in the far opening and had begun firing long bursts down across the shallow footholds leading up to their positions. Chandler, Sewell, and Collins covered the backs of their heads with crossed forearms, and pressed themselves flatter against the ledge.

"Pull back!" they could barely hear Ross shouting up to them above the roar of automatic weapons fire—two more MG nests had hastily been slapped together, and the bandit gang was slowly converging three separate streams of lead down against the middle of the cliff. The lieutenant was yelling in Spanish again. "We appear to be outgunned and the element of surprise eluded us from the start!"

He's got his gall using so many words in the middle of a firefight, Chandler thought to himself as he readied another magazine of rounds. He eased it into the bottom of his weapon and slapped it tightly in place until he heard it click home.

"For this crap we don't get enough pay!" Ross was still yelling up at them between carefully spaced bursts of tracer from the ground. "Better to break off contact now, lads . . . so we can return to fight another day!"

Chandler couldn't help but get the feeling Ross sounded drunk on adrenalin—*high on gunsmoke!* The thought made him grin to himself, despite the minute slivers of ricocheting lead peppering his limbs from all directions. *Damned bastard's got his nerve: preachin' like that from the safety of the ground....*

"And how do you propose we retreat at this time?" Sewell responded at the top of his lungs, also in Spanish. "The same way we came up!?"

"Improvise!" The army officer's tone was full of encouragement, but all three men on the ledge detected the smile on his lips.

"Improvise?" Sewell swallowed dryly as he glanced over at Collins. Chandler was staring out at the rope they had used to climb up to the ledge leading to the footholds—or what was left of it. The bottom twenty feet had been cut away by crisscrossing waves of bullets.

But the Americans weren't forced to improvise.

Just as it began to seem the clearing within the rain forest—already dense with gunsmoke and tear gas—would be unable to contain any more exploding discharges, laserlike streams of bright red tracer lanced up at the three cave openings from a dozen different points on either side of Lieutenant Ross.

Within moments, the entire wall of limestone around the entrances was alive with bright sparks of glowing particles that drove the bandits deeper into the bowels of the earth.

Startled by the unexpected assistance from within the dark jungle and shadow-laced tree line, Ross directed his attention back up at his team.

"Make your way back down!" he shouted, both fists clenched as Collins's sniper rifle dangled against one side and his submachine gun the other. "Now!"

"'Now' he says!" Collins mimicked the lieutenant sarcastically, as he bolted to his feet and started back down the ledge to where it abruptly ended. He quickly made the decision to leap into the tree branches ten feet below. Without the rope, it was the only way down.

"I'm right behind you!" Sewell warned as the men raced along the narrow edge. Collins gave the thumbs-up as encouragement while Chandler brought up the rear, confident a stray round would punch in the back of his skull and slam him off his feet any second.

Before jumping into the mangled branches of the smaller trees below, he glanced back one last time at all the shafts of tracer light being directed up at the cave openings from a dozen different locations. The sight was beautiful . . . mesmerizing.

"*Run*, you crazy bastards," Ross muttered under his breath as another flare exploded against the cliff wall and arced back toward the ground—its parachute torn free—like some spectacular falling star.

A stirring in the trees behind him made Ross tense but he did not immediately turn around. He knew it was Princess Raina with her soldiers—he had detected her memorable perfume moments after shadows on the ground had begun firing up at the tunnels to protect his men. When she put her hand on his waist, moving closer, he smiled, still watching his men the whole time. "When you hear the pitter patter of clumsy feet. . . ." he whispered.

Princess Raina responded, warm lips brushing against his ear, "It's Roscoe's Raiders in full retreat. . . ."

"You shoulda been there, Cory," Collins bragged later, as the group of Khmers and Americans sat around a huge campfire much later, at predawn. "I mean, we were really kicking ass, brother! Perched on a narrow ledge, tossing grenades in on 'em left and right, dodging slugs from three different points of fire—it was beautiful!"

"*Shit*," Matt Sewell muttered quietly from the other side of the flames.

"From what I hear," MacArthur masked his intense relief at seeing his friends' safe return with a taunting grin, "you clowns barely escaped with your asses dragging."

Sentries were positioned at points surrounding the gathering, but few worried the bandit gang would regroup or venture out of their caves so soon. Ross's team had not routed them, as planned, but the arrival of Princess Raina's reinforcements had served to hit the Chinese with a demoralizing blow that no doubt had left scores injured; you couldn't unleash that much flak at a hole in the wall without a lot of people sustaining serious wounds, if only from ricochets.

A log in the middle of the campfire, green and wet as were most slabs they had dragged in from the depths of the rain forest, exploded loudly as the heat boiled the water inside to the bursting point. Glowing embers spiraled into the humid night air, and as hot ash took to the breeze, Collins peeled himself back up off the ground.

"Only a log, Brent," Princess Raina laughed lightly, hoping not to embarrass him. "Only a log...."

Ross moved his fingers through a large vat of sticky rice and rolled the white paste into a small ball. He took a tamarind leaf from his bamboo plate and dipped it into the bowl of *prahoc*, then sprinkled the fish sauce over the rice. The pungent aroma tickled his nostrils, and Princess Raina smiled approvingly as he took a large bite. For Ross, it was not an act or courtesy; he loved the stuff.

"I'm afraid, once again, we didn't accomplish what we set out to—"

But the princess silenced him with the usual two fingers pressed quickly against his lips. "I was pleasantly surprised at how well our two teams—working together—beat back the Chinese. The most serious casualty on our side suffered only from burns caused when a flying brass cartridge landed within his shirt collar.

"We work well together, Justin," she continued, lowering her voice as she snuggled closer to him. Ross glanced down at the unflattering sampot skirt she had wrapped around her body. Where it was folded along the top, against her breasts, the fabric was coming loose, and she did nothing to tighten it back into place. The effect was driving Ross wild, but he hid all emotion. "It is too bad you choose not to stay on with us," she said. "We could eventually graduate from beating back unprofessional hoodlums to—with your guidance—ambushing the Communists again...."

"But—"

"But, of course, your duty calls." She looked up at him, unsmiling now, and Ross stared into the flames, suddenly sad.

He wanted to yell *Fuck it!* at the night. He wanted to stand up, to tell Collins to send a *Screw you!* cable to Mr. Y back at the Pentagon. He wanted to lift the princess off her feet, swirl her around in front of the men and all the animal eyes watching from the forest shadows, and drag her off to their waterfall—not to be seen again for weeks.

But he just kept staring into the campfire.

Somewhere deep in the jungle an old panther screamed up at the stars, and Ross wondered if it had recently lost its mate—the sound was so mournful . . . so sad—or if it had always prowled the rain forests on its own. He watched the faint glow along the east wall of trees signal the coming of dawn, and he knew it was time to drag the radio—and not the princess—off through the jungle, toward the highest peak to the north. But it was Chandler who finally spoke, breaking the spell of the crackling embers.

"Time for us to be moving, Lieutenant," he said softly. Collins and Sewell slowly got to their feet, shaking off cramps as if they were just emerging from ten hours in a sleeping bag. Cory remained beside the fire, eyes locked on those of a young woman who had been attending him in recent days. He was not going to budge. Not for anybody, or so he kept telling himself.

Ross glanced at his wristwatch.

"Transmission is in three-five," Chandler reminded him, shouldering the portable radio. Communications had been Amy's specialty, and since her absence, they had been trading off with the heavy equipment. Ross felt it served to instill in the men an appreciation for all the months the woman had fielded the cumbersome sets without complaint.

"We'd better get moving," he agreed. Then, to himself: If we don't check in on schedule, the clowns back at Disneyland East will have this quadrant of the country crawling with spook-suits.

"You'll be returning from the mountaintop?" Princess Raina asked him as she too stood up. Her eyes pleaded for only one response. "Or will you leave directly on your . . . mission?"

"I can't answer that right now," Ross raised his voice so that all the Khmers could hear him. "But I can promise you one thing: Lady Luck willing, we shall return, Your Highness." The princess flinched at the title, and Ross could tell that had so many of her people not been watching she would have kicked him in the shins. "We did not finish what we set out to do here . . . we did not accomplish our mission here in this valley. . . ."

"You rescued me!" the princess's brother said, stepping forward from the rest of the men crowding around.

"A lucky break," Ross conceded, "but we did not permanently alleviate the problem facing your people."

"After tonight," the young man rubbed his fingers against the string of shriveled ears around his neck in reflection, "I don't think the cave bandits will pose much of a problem, sir."

"Nevertheless," Chandler said, starting toward the

hills leading up out of the jungle—he knew they could stay there till high noon if they didn't quit jawing soon—"we'll return to check on you when we can."

"I guarantee it," Ross added.

A hundred hands silently clapping them on the back as they passed through the Cambodians, Ross's team left the camp as the first shafts of dim light cut through the rain forest gloom and descended through the smoky mist.

And they climbed.

Across two low ranges and halfway up the summit of the highest peak in the region, they moved, not halting until they could look down on the calm stretch of green, misty jungle they had just left, swirls of smoke from the Khmer campfires still faintly visible. The scene stretching out before him made Ross sad: he felt like he was abandoning his own people . . . his own ancestors *and* future descendents, yet a gnawing in his gut also told him these were not his brothers and sisters at all, but a race of jungle dwellers so different from himself in so many ways that he could never dream to identify with them. They came from races divided by an entire ocean— never mind the sea of trees—and Ross could never really hope to fit in, even if he chose a woman like Raina to live beside him.

"Nothin' but static," Chandler complained, even though he had just set up the whip antenna. "We're just gonna have to hoof it on back to Saigontown, Justin. Otherwise—"

But there came a sudden series of multi-pitch tones even as he spoke, and both Ross and Collins started frantically copying the coded message down. "Well, fuck *me*," Chandler muttered as he tuned the frequency in clearer, then locked it on channel.

Three minutes later, after the message had been repeated once using a secondary code, the transmission ended.

"Do we decode it here," Sewell glanced about the mountainside. "Or work on it back down there in the trees?"

Ross wiped sweat from his brow with the back of his hand and checked the sun's progress. The temperature had to be approaching a hundred and ten in the shade. The team hadn't worked codes in ages—it could take a long time to figure out what he was sure would be two-and-a-half minutes of reprimanding ramblings from old man Y, followed by thirty seconds of mission directives. They could just as easily listen to all that from under the cover of the trees, where it would be somewhat cooler, but Ross didn't wish to return to the princess's camp. One good-bye had been painful enough.

"Get to work on it," he said, handing his notebook to Sewell. The expression on his face told the men he was climbing a few meters higher for a little reflective solitude.

"I've already got it decoded," Collins said. He had been furiously scribbling across his notebook and the announcement came as a matter-of-fact statement, with complete absence of pride or satisfaction. "The first two minutes is nothing but crap to throw off anyone listening in."

"You're sure?" Ross sat back down.

"Positive. They sent it out so it'd sound like simple

electronics shadows put out by any aircraft flying over the area... the kinda stuff a commercial airliner would transmit routinely...."

"Get to the meat," Cory said, his mood irritable as he made a show of dragging his leg painfully around.

"They're sending us back into Vietnam," Collins finally revealed.

"Home sweet home," Sewell replied sarcastically.

"So what else is new?" Chandler said as he set about oiling down his rifle.

"We're to deploy outside a place called Katum... seven klicks to the west, to be precise."

"Katum?" Sewell repeated the name. "Doesn't sound remotely Vietnamese to me."

"It is," Ross cut in, his mind flashing back to some incident in his past as he pulled out a acetone-marked map. "About twenty-five kilometers to the whiskey of An Loc. Surrounded on three sides by gaping jaws of Cambodian territory." He hoped he wasn't sounding too dramatic, but the men didn't seem to be listening that carefully anyway—they were all drenched in sweat, miserable, and sinking in silent, self-pity. "The place is bad news," Ross continued. "Heavy concentrations of Vietcong, and even on-again off-again reports of hardcore NVA. What's the mission?"

"There's an American P.O.W. camp supposed to be there, Justin."

The men all immediately perked up, their interest whetted.

"P.O.W.s?" Ross sounded incredulous. "There?"

"That's what the message says."

"But Katum is only a stone's throw from Saigon!"

"They expect *us?*" Sewell gestured around to each man in the group, especially Cory, who was still heavily bandaged but able to function on his own now, "they expect *us* to rescue a bunch of marines or whatever from a prison camp?"

"Why don't they send in a detachment of Green Berets or something?" Cory protested, the pain in his leg suddenly throbbing with the thought of mounting a ground assault on a heavily defended stockade.

"Because they don't want us to rescue anyone," Ross stated confidently, his words silencing the others. He knew the purpose of the team was not search and rescue, but search and *destroy*.

"Correct," Collins said, staring down at the ground, his features grim.

"I don't get it," MacArthur slipped his rifle sling off his shoulder, pulled a tiny can of gun oil from its stock compartment, and began imitating Chandler.

"There's an American lieutenant the VC got in one of their torture chambers," Collins swallowed hard. "We're to slip in and terminate him. On the spot. No questions asked."

5.

Chad Chandler pulled the cartridges slowly out of the rifle magazine for the third time, carefully checked the clip's innerspring mechanism, examined each bullet individually, then began replacing them into the narrow metal banana. He appeared to be ignoring all the talk going on between the others, but in fact he was listening intently to each word, just as he was cautiously checking each cartridge for deformities or damage. It was a green recruit who entered battle with poorly maintained equipment: sudden death often followed the unforgivable jamming of one's weapon on the battlefield. And it was an undisciplined rookie who did not absorb each word in a pre-op briefing.

Though Chandler knew that each round going into his rifle was now immaculate, and though he missed nothing the men were saying, his mind was miles away, scanning brilliant memories from another country that hadn't faded with age.

"It would be nice if we had a picture of the man," Collins complained, refusing to dwell on the morals of sniping out one of his own kind.

"I'll wager our target will be the only round-eye in the camp," Ross said. "I've heard rumors of this interrogation center before. Uncle Sammy has sent troops in there hoping to flush out the Cong in the past, but they've got a tunnel system that's hard to crack. Some of the top brass back at Puzzle Palace have even said publicly they doubt it exists . . . that it's only legend, created by bored ARVNs conjuring up action around their campfires at night. The camp is only used for quickie rap sessions, before soldiers recently captured can be marched further into the jungle, across the border into Cambodia, to the big monkey house rumored to be hidden somewhere near Prey Veng. The only other round-eyes we'll probably see are Eastern Bloc advisors. . . ."

"And they're open season?" Collins rubbed his sniper rifle like it was a woman's thigh.

"After the mission goes down," Ross replied, "the whole damned joint is a free-fire zone, Brent."

"Well, I'd like to go over the dude's description again, anyway," said Cory. "Just to play it safe."

"We always play it safe around here, my friend . . . you know that. . . ." MacArthur snorted loudly, scratching the itch that had erupted under his leg bandages. "Anyway, I'll go over it again."

Ross compared his notepad with Collins's. There was no discrepancy in the message they had decoded. "Our man's caucasian, six foot, one hundred eighty pounds—prior to his capture anyway, blond hair, green eyes, with a crucifix scar along the small of his back and another where his appendix used to be. He's an air force second-louie, shot down sixty seconds after taking off from the Bien Hoa air base. Captured alive ten klicks west of the air base. Last name Pruitt. First name Jonathan. Date of birth, 1944—that would make him twenty years old now. He's been in custody shortly longer than a week, so he probably only looks thirty by now."

Chandler didn't smile at the grim humor like the rest of the men in the team. He was rubbing the rifle stock harder, heating up the gun oil as he polished the dark woodgrain. Ross watched him for a few seconds, curious—it looked like the weapon might burst into flames at any moment. He almost asked his demolitions expert what was on his mind, but by now Ross knew he wouldn't get a straight answer, so he remained silent. Watching.

Chandler would normally have noticed the team leader's watchful gaze, but all he saw now was that icy battlefield thirteen years earlier in Korea. It was the last time he had seen Second Lieutenant Pruitt's father alive.

"Why exactly are we bustin' our balls to cancel this guy's ticket, anyway?" Sewell asked Ross. "Is he on the war crimes list or something?"

"A man after my own heart," Collins cut in.

"I mean, does he hold some secret information they're afraid the Commies will be able to torture out of him or something?"

"I'll bet he was a double agent," MacArthur sat up straight as the possibility hit him. "Got caught stealing a Phantom or something and they blasted his ass out of the sky right as he lifted off from the runway. Didn't get the aircraft over the border to the enemy, but the brass opted to waste him anyway, for the hell of it. . . ."

"It's the principle of the thing," Collins agreed.

"What's the scoop, Roscoe?" Sewell persisted, sensing the lieutenant didn't want to talk.

"You clowns know the rules," was his simple response.

"Aw, come on, Justin," cooed Cory. "Don't be an asshole."

Collins's shoulders drooped slightly at the disrespectful reference and the flak that was sure to follow, but Ross was not quick to shoot a retort.

"Yah, Lieutenant," Sewell soothed the wound with the use of military rank. But Ross didn't consider himself a company man: the ploy did not work.

"I can't go into particulars—you know how we operate around here," he interrupted himself. "We get our orders, we carry out the mission, then we disperse and regroup across the border, awaiting the next op . . . *no questions asked.*"

"But we're talking an *American* here!" Sewell pressed into dangerous territory, ignoring the warning signals in Ross's eyes.

"You watched me when the message came in," Ross said defensively. "I didn't get any more information than you did. How am I supposed to answer your questions if that's the case?"

"We didn't go traipsing up here into Cambodia just to try and seduce some top-heavy princess," Sewell lashed back. "Somehow, you knew about this mission all along. The problems with Raina's brother just happened to work out to fit your needs." Sewell's expression took on a crafty gleam, and despite his anger, there was the hint of admiration in his eyes. "It don't take no logistics expert to surmise the best way to hit this so-called interrogation center would be from the west—over the border right out of Cambodia. That's a Communist stronghold, gentlemen. The dinks wouldn't be expecting anything other than a few above-the-clouds recon planes from that direction, much less a crack commando unit like ourselves," he breathed on his fingernails dramatically and scratched the harsh fabric over his heart in mocking self-admiration.

"Come on, Justin," Cory persisted. "Level with us. Level with us, or this punk ain't budging an inch from the side of this mountain," and he folded his arms across his chest as if to accent his point.

Chandler wasn't really listening to the arguments any more. He was thinking back to the three meetings he had had with the young air force officer.

The first had been five years earlier, when Chad himself had, out of curiosity, journeyed across midwest America to visit the wife of the man he had fought beside in Korea. After Johnny Pruitt had turned up missing in action, Chandler had grieved, spending several months angry at the world, then had gone on with his life, never really thinking much about his friend's family back in the States.

Then he had received the lengthy letter from Pruitt's son, fifteen-year-old Jonathan Paul. A testament to a boy's love for a father he had never really known . . . except through faded photographs in an old soldier's trunk his mother had kept hidden for as many years in the attic. The letter was almost twenty pages long, and after getting over the initial shock at how the kid had managed to track him down despite the passage of so many years, Chandler marveled at the youth's ability to put into words a description of a man that was so very accurate—even though the soldier-father had died . . . no, disappeared during a firefight when the boy was only seven years old.

The last page of the letter was the one that had really disturbed Chad, however. It spoke of dreams the teenager was having. Troubled nightmares where he saw his father alive, held somewhere against his will. Patiently waiting for his fellow soldiers to rescue him . . . for the day when he could see his wife and son again.

But the Korean War had ended long ago, and the United States Army had never located Johnny Pruitt or the sentry who had disappeared alongside him during the intense climax of that battle for Camp Starburst.

The second encounter with the boy had been when Chandler was working as a ranch hand in Africa. Although he had written letters back to his army buddies during this period telling them he was a mercenary ravaging melon-chested black women in Rhodesia, the two years had really been spent protecting a rancher's cows from rustlers, and he had actually been nothing more than a security guard.

The boy's mother had tracked him down that time, checking with her husband's army buddies until she'd found one who knew he was chasing adventure and elusive paychecks across the dark continent. She had written telling about her son's obsession with finding his father, and Chandler had finally agreed to talk with him again—if only to burst his bubble and get him to face reality: his father was probably buried beneath the charred structures that had once been Camp Starburst. The boy's mother had not been able to afford the airfare to Rhodesia, and when Chandler had explained he was on the verge of moving into beggar's row himself, she had opted for sending her son by boat, hoping a couple of weeks on the high seas would not only serve to awaken the youth about the realities of the world, but that a few storm-driven waves would drown his thirst for adventure away from home.

When the boy had finally arrived on the plains of the Macheke badlands, though, he was not in the least downtrodden or disenchanted. In fact, he had taken to wearing cool African garb, and talked constantly of hunting safaris the first two days.

"I know my father is probably dead," he had finally admitted one evening at dusk, after they had spent eighteen hours pursuing a tiger through the bush. The animal had stayed ahead of them the entire day, and—as was always the case when Chad was guarding the rancher's livestock—they could hear the big cat roaring at them in challenge, could follow its tracks along the soft ground, but could never actually see the animal. "I realize he probably died without firing a shot when the Chinese hit you guys with everything they had that day...."

"It was hell," Chandler had recalled, his eyes glazing over as he relived the ferocity of the sudden ambush ten years earlier. "Your father was carrying a wounded soldier over his back. He died a hero, son. He deserved—"

"My gut tells me dad is alive," the youth had said,

biting his lower lip with determination, but I'm not sure I can stomach chasing this tragedy the rest of my life. The clues ran out long ago."

"Yes...."

"The clues regarding my father, anyway," young Pruitt had said as he put down the skewer holding the three lizard torsos and locked eyes with Chandler. "You survived the ambush, Mr. Chandler. You and one other man."

Chandler's eyes had narrowed as he recalled—with crystal clarity—the sleeping sentry's face as he had practically stumbled over him. "The guard was also missing," he had said somberly, deciding not to go into particulars—like how all these years Chandler had wanted to bust the soldier to buck private for sleeping on duty, and to brand his personnel file with the worst label possible . . . next to deserter.

"His name was Jefferson," the boy had shot the words out like an accusation. "Jefferson, Leon J. He's alive, Mr. Chandler. He's been spotted in the North Korean capital—"

"He's a P.O.W.?"

"I doubt that," Jonathan had said sarcastically, hatred in his tone. "I've got news clips that show him supervising a farm conservation project. I've seen documents that would lead one to believe he roams North Korea without restrictions . . . that he has an Asian wife . . . that he travels throughout the eastern bloc nations—"

"*A turncoat!?*" Chandler had exploded, sending several birds nesting in nearby bush into hectic flight.

But Jonathan had calmly gone silent. He'd picked

the skewer back up, rolled it through the flames a few more times, then had angrily torn one of the lizards off with his teeth.

After he had swallowed it and had drunk from Chandler's liquor pouch, he revealed, "I hold little hope of seeing my father alive again, Mr. Chandler. I doubt he is being kept in a North Korean prison camp somewhere, and his rank was not high enough, in my opinion, to justify moving him from country to country as a showpiece, propaganda tool, or source of military intelligence." Chandler was awed by the boy's ability to talk so decisively even after two canteens of bourbon.

"What, then?" the liquor had begun to work on Chad by then, and his head had flopped to the side, his eyes staring straight up at the brilliant silver moon clearing the horizon.

"Revenge," the kid had said, admitting what Chandler had suspected all along. "This Jefferson character could have helped save my father. He could have stayed to fight with you and the others, but instead he chose to run . . . and later on conspire with the enemy—"

"Now we don't really know that for a fact," Chandler had pointed out, coming to the defense of a man he had dreamed of killing with his bare hands a hundred times over. "He might have gotten captured, son. They might have tortured his ass into submission . . . coerced him into cooperating . . . it could be—"

"*Bullshit!*" Jonathan had jumped up, knocking over a burning log from the campfire in the process, the glowing embers taking to the wind, swirling about the men like enchanted forest pixies. "That son of a bitch holds the key to my peace of mind, mister . . . and I'm not going to rest until I have the answer to this—"

"And what do you propose to do, kind sir?" Chandler had interrupted, crossing his legs, getting comfortable as if preparing for a lengthy explanation. "I'm all ears. If I can help you, in *any* way, I'll be the first to jump on the bandwagon, Jonathan. I just think you're fighting a losing battle. . . ."

"Like you and my dad fought. . . ."

Chandler had lowered his head in somber reflection, feeling butterflies chasing each other about in his stomach now. "Yah, I guess so," he had said after a few moments of silence. "Like your father and I fought. . . ."

"I'm sweet sixteen," the kid had said, his admission soaked in sarcasm and sudden maturity. "What can I do? You—you're a man. A man who fought beside my father! Don't you feel some sort of brothership . . . some sort of allegiance . . . some loyalty?"

"Yes. . . ."

"You *owe* him, Mr. Chandler! You *owe* him!" Jonathan had been on the verge of tears.

"Tell me what I can do to help," he had replied slowly, his voice cracking this time. "I've lived through that battle in my mind a hundred-thousand times . . . I've critiqued it endlessly, and there's nothing anyone can do to change it. I ran out of solutions long ago, son. Tell me what I can do to help now. . . ."

"*I'm* the kid here," Jonathan had said, finally

breaking down and sobbing, reaching out to pound a fist in the campfire ash. "*You're* supposed to tell *me* what to do!"

But Chandler had not been able to come up with an answer, and the next morning the boy had disappeared.

Not that concerned for the kid's safety, but more out of curiosity, he had checked with the officials in the city: Jonathan Paul Pruitt had taken the predawn flight back to New York City.

Their third and final meeting had been in Saigon only a few months ago . . .

Chandler and the others were celebrating in a Tu Do Street bar after terminating a rather outspoken American superstar with liberal convictions. Some MPs had just completed a routine check of the establishment, (giving team leader Ross the evil eye and thumbs-up compliment at the same time), when the younger Pruitt sauntered in, an Australian bush hat concealing the left side of his face as he bought Ross's table a round of drinks.

But Ross's demo man had recognized the kid immediately, and they soon embraced in a bear hug their fragile friendship did not really warrant. That was Saigon for you, though. Men did funny things because of the war.

"What the hell is this?" Chandler had spotted the airman's shirt beneath the improvised safari suit. "Been outta my sight a couple lousy years and some wing nut recruiter done wrestled away your virginity. . . ."

"I was sort of wondering what exactly brought *you* into these parts also, Chad. Last I saw of you—"

"Last I saw of *you*, you were hoppin' a cropduster back to The World, boy," he said ignoring the officer's rank. "I always wanted to ask you where you mysteriously came up with the money for the plane ticket—your mama-san barely had enough to buy you boat fare."

"I had some rainy-day money stashed away in my sock," Jonathan said slyly. "No need to tell the old lady about everything."

"Hmphhh...." Chandler dragged him away from the others and guided him over to the deserted side of the bar counter.

"That 'cropduster' ride back really got me interested in airplanes and flight. I busted my balls at the books and lucked out; got into the good old USAF... imagine that—Jonathan Pruitt behind the stick of a jet fighter...."

Chandler ignored the display of modesty covered by sweet icing. "You come from good stock," he said.

"Yah." The kid's eyes fell to the floor and his smile faded. "That's why I'm here."

"You're not *stationed* in the 'Nam?" Chandler asked incredulously.

"No. Utapao, over in Thailand. Near Sattahip."

"And you just happened to take your R & R in the Pearl of the Orient," Chandler sounded skeptical.

"Thirty days leave," Pruitt corrected him softly.

Chandler draped a heavy, brotherly arm around the officer's shoulder. "Okay, kid. Let me have it with both barrels. Don't try fuckin' me in the ear either—I was born at night, but not *last* night!"

"I'm still on the trail of the man who shares the Missing In Action roster with my father."

"I figured as much," Chandler said, producing a deep frown as he waved to the bartender at the other end of the counter.

Jukebox music was playing in the smoky background—a melodic Diana Ross and The Supremes hit currently topping the charts back home—two dancers swaying back and forth to the rhythm, in cages suspended from the ceiling. Clad in string bikinis, they looked fresh off the farm.

The bartender, also a woman, looked ten years older than the dancers, and her eyes radiated an icyness that had taken three wars to cultivate. "What's your pleasure, Mac?" she stared up at Chandler out of the corners of both eyes, a tired grimace across her lips—the total expression told both men they had better not be wasting her time with unnecessary sweet talk.

"Another bourbon." Chandler was not impressed with the hardcore mask. If she wasn't careful he'd slap it off her.

"And you, cherry-boy?" She smacked a mouthful of bubblegum at Pruitt. Chandler swallowed hard—the sudden crack in the air seemed more like an act of violence than anything, and it reminded him of poor Amy, recuperating somewhere miles away, alone.

"This *boy* is a fucking lieutenant in the United States Air Force, *miss*!" Chandler reached out and grabbed the bartender's arm. "He's out there all day risking life and limb for you and yours so this lousy country can—"

"Just a Seven-Up," Pruitt raised a hand between

them, requesting peace, but the woman refused to mellow-out: Chandler had stepped on a tiger's tail.

"Spare me the sermon, Mister Wonderful!" she said, staring past the airman and locking eyes with Chandler. "I lost my whole family during the French-Vietminh War! I work in this bar since I was old enough to spread my legs for the owner! My child die under a napalm attack one year ago this week! So please excuse me if I fail to show great deal respect for American, French, or *any* foreign uniform!" But then her eyes softened and she whirled around to leave. "One bourbon and one Seven-Up *coming* up."

"Jesus," Chandler whispered after she was out of hearing range. "The fucking help these days is always on the warpath."

Pruitt ignored him, staring up at one of the dancers seemingly helpless in her bamboo cage. Multicolored floor lights sent shafts of purple and crimson up through the dense cigarette smoke to play about on her curves as she moved along with the beat of the stereo speakers.

Chandler waved a hand in front of his eyes. "Got yourself one of them tealocks back at Utapao?" he tried to break Pruitt's concentration.

"No." The answer came as if an officer's honor was suddenly in question, and the second lieutenant quickly looked away. "I have a fiancée back in the States."

"I hear tell them Thai women are the most beautiful in the world, lad. It'd be hard to resist a reputation like that—what with an officer's paycheck like yours coming in at the end of each month...."

Chandler himself kept his eyes on the nearest dancer. She was shedding her sparkling top now, and when it was free, she turned her back on the tables at the front of the bar and began swaying her hips about sensually. Several patrons began loud groans of protest while others applauded. The latter were obviously leg men, the others chest fanatics—who had just been teased beyond the limit.

"Crazy cunt's gonna cause a riot," Chandler's tone was nothing but admiration as he watched the muscular thighs shift about in the narrow shafts of light. The Chinese lanterns in every corner of the room went slowly out, and when strobes began shooting blasts of silver light against the dancers, the women were totally nude, their routine now becoming more wild as the scene in front of the customers began to look like a movie show with every second and third frame missing.

"Quite a show, Big Chad . . . you come here often?" Pruitt was no longer watching the women, but staring down at his knuckles.

"Never on Sunday, J.P. . . . Never on Sunday. . . ."

The bartender did not return but slid their glasses down the smooth counter instead. Propelled with just the right amount of force, they slid to a stop directly in front of both Americans.

"And what—if I might be so bold to ask—brings you to South Vietnam?" Pruitt gave Chandler an accusing look. "That motley group you hang out with over there looks a bit suspicious, if one were to ask me. . . ."

Well, no one's asking you, Chandler wanted to reply, but he said instead, "Imports-exports, J.P. It's where the money's at these days."

"Imports-exports?" The young lieutenant cast him a skeptical smile. "Isn't that the classic cloak-and-dagger response? Sounds rather clandestine to me."

"Rubber, sugarcane, war brides," Chandler mused. "This place has got it all. I expect to make my fortune long before the Viets kick us out of the country the way they booted the lousy French."

"Any room for a rookie pilot?" He sounded genuinely interested.

"Keep those butter bars on your collar, J.P." Chandler frowned. "The business *I'm* in has little job security. You could be on the verge of locating that legendary pot of gold on the far side of the rainbow, or you could be a hair's breadth away from a smuggler's bullet. At least *you* can count on a pension. And health insurance if some sailor breaks your jaw in a barroom brawl."

"Sounds like you could use a bona-fide bush pilot," the airman persisted, ignoring the bad points.

"Enough about me and my pursuits," Chandler said, turning the "interview" around again. "I'm concerned about *you*, Jonathan. When are you going to give up this obsession about what happened in Korea over a decade ago? It's all going to get you nothing but an ulcer and a sharp reduction in the number of loyal friends that'll stand by you in times of—"

"The bastard is here, Chad," he said coldly, the grin completely gone.

"Who?"

"The black man who disappeared with my father."

"Time for another drink, son." But Pruitt reached out and grabbed his wrist, preventing the bigger man from summoning the bartender.

"He's here in Vietnam somewhere. Perhaps Hanoi . . . perhaps—"

"Hanoi?" Chandler shook his head from side to side. "What would he be doing in Hanoi?"

"I'm unable to locate any confirmed sightings by any of our people over the last ten years," he admitted, "but I've been scanning Communist documents and newspapers every chance I get."

"And you've spotted his likeness in news photos."

"Not his likeness! It's him. The same evidence is in all the photos: a jagged scar on his left cheek. I've placed him in East Germany, Cuba, North Korea, even Peking."

Chandler's mind raced back to that morning in the frozen trench along the Camp Starburst perimeter. When he had slammed his fist into the sentry's face, leaving a deep gash.

"And my latest research puts him at a jungle supply point along the Ho Chi Minh trail," the lieutenant continued.

"Impossible." Chandler let the word escape his lips as he gauged the chances this young officer beside him was right.

"I'm not saying the guy's a guerilla. It's bigger than that. I believe he's risen through the Party ranks over the years and now goes from country to country, inspecting Communist groundwork in Asia—sort of like an advisor, if you will. . . ."

"I can't buy that, J.P.," Chandler objected to the theory quietly. "He'd be much too valuable as a propaganda showpiece. You know—negro soldier revolts against repressive American military system to join the underground liberation movement, et cetera, et cetera. . . ."

Their conversation began to fizzle out. "Nobody has actually seen the man in person in nearly a decade, according to your own research. Your theory's got too many holes in it. Too many 'ifs.' It's not worth throwing your career away over."

"The taste of job satisfaction grows sour quickly, Big Chad, when you hang up your flight gear and go home to a house filled with reminders of betrayal and abandonment. . . ."

"I said it's time to move out," Justin Ross nudged him on the shoulder. Chandler whirled his head around, quickly focusing on the squad leader—the strobe lights, nude dancers, and stereo music of the dark Tu Do Street bar suddenly vanished, and he began breathing the sweet scent of the rain forest instead of dense cigarette smoke.

Clouds were passing a stone's throw away as they floated around the jutting mountain peak. Below, a vast panorama of brilliant green jungle spread out before him. A slight wisp of silver marked the spot where the Khmers were camping beneath the thick canopy.

"No."

Ross and the others halted moments after starting

down the steep trail. "What?" The lieutenant did not sound shocked, but mildly irritated by the delay—and the arguments he sensed were forthcoming.

"I'm not moving from this spot." Chandler sounded serious.

"Well awright!" Cory shook a clenched fist in the thin air. "A mountaintop monk right here in our irreverent midst!" He fell to his knees and began worshiping Chad with outstretched arms, lowering his bowed head to the ground.

"Come on, Chandler," Sewell muttered. "We're wasting time."

"I'm not going."

"He's not going," young Cory jumped in front of Ross, mock seriousness in his innocent eyes as he waved a hand in Chandler's direction like some ancient court jester.

"Oh, he's going," Ross spoke in his most confident tone. "We're *all* going. Home to Vietnam, boys!" He raised his own fist in the mist, hoping the attempt at peer psychology would work.

"I got a little Cambodian chick down there who'll treat me like lord and master," Chandler said, rocking back and forth on his heels as he squatted, hands grasping the outcropping of rock beneath his feet as if preparing to spring out at them. His eyes darted from side to side, watching everything. "She'll walk on my back, feed me, screw me, bathe me—do anything my jollies demand!"

"I do declare," Cory danced circles around Chad as he put the words to music, "the mountaintop bonze is on Cloud Nine! The mountaintop bonze is on Cloud Nine!"

Chandler and Ross both ignored him. "I just can't see following you guys back into another shitstorm, Justin. This little valley is paradise, and you know it."

"The war will eventually find its way here, Chad. You know that. Hell, already the 'crime rate,' if you wanna call it that, has soared higher than some hilltops in the Bronx—what with those Chinese banditos the scourge of the countryside."

Chandler did not buy the comparison. "I can handle them," he said. "Especially after last night."

"Yah," Sewell let his lips slip loose. "I imagine Lu-long's boys will be keepin' to themselves for some time to come. . . ."

Ross cast his chopper pilot an irritated scowl. He was fast losing his sense of humor. "Let's go," he said, staring directly into Chandler's eyes. Then he turned his back on the man and started down the trail.

"I told you," the ex-mercenary started to say, "I'm not—"

But when Ross whirled back around to face him, the army lieutenant had his pistol out. "I explained to you when you came aboard," he said slowly, "that this cruise was for the duration, Chandler. You're a soldier in my army. You play by my rules. You follow my orders. Now I'm ordering you to get up off your ass and accompany us down this anthill. Then you're going to follow us into combat—wherever our mission takes us." He did not aim the pistol, but kept it at waist level, directly in front of him. The barrel was trained on Chandler's face. "Is that clear?"

Big Chad locked eyes with Ross, and then he stared

into the black tunnel of the barrel. He thought about young Jonathan Pruitt sitting in a cell west of Katum, and about their orders to penetrate the camp and terminate him. He thought about the air force lieutenant's lifelong search for the sentry who had disappeared alongside his father from a Korean trench years earlier. And he decided then and there it just might be worth it to venture back into South Vietnam—if only to see how the pieces in the mystery puzzle fell into place.

"Is that clear?" Ross repeated the question.

"And if I refuse?"

"Then you can remain on this mountaintop," Ross conceded, "*forever*. Because after I splatter your spongy excuse for brains across those flowers back there, me and the boys here will commence to scattering your arms, legs, and head all over the place, chump. And you *know* Khmer legend has it that—"

"Youse guys would do that to me?" Chandler cut him off as he looked at each man in turn, betrayal and hurt in his moist eyes.

"Orders is orders, Big Chad." Sewell flashed an ear-to-ear set of gleaming teeth as he slowly drew his machete from its sheath on his web belt.

Sewell was joking. Ross was not.

"Nothing personal." Cory produced his Swiss army knife and flipped out the corkscrew. In reverent silence, he began acting as if he were drilling it into his ear.

"What's it going to be?" Ross pulled the hammer back on the K-54 Russian automatic.

Chandler's eyes crossed slightly as he tried to focus

on the lieutenant's knuckles. He swallowed hard, then slowly rose to his feet. Cautiously, he brought his right hand up into a casual salute.

Without further conversation, Ross holstered his pistol, and the five Americans started back down the mountainside.

6.

The men glanced back at the rapidly fading lights from the village one last time, then threw their shoulders into their work and paddled.

Brilliant bolts of lightning split the black sky above, and a cool breeze chased them down the Song May River as they crossed the Cambodian border into South Vietnam. Huge raindrops pelted them now and then as their raft passed through sheets of the monsoon storm.

"Paddle faster!" Ross's harsh whisper cut through the roar of the narrow river, easily carrying to the other four men in the small craft. "Faster!"

The Americans complied silently, choosing the current carefully—aiming for the glowing silver spurs that marked the rapids, then veering alongside them at the last moment for that extra surge of speed.

Lieutenant Ross didn't need to elaborate. Every man present knew the fury of the storm could serve to distract the enemy from their arrival. The problem was that the storm seemed to be moving north by northwest. And they were heading in the opposite direction. They could only hope it was an all-night affair, and not one of the more common midnight barrages the skies sucked in from the restless Gulf of Siam.

Chandler—the lead man in the craft—checked his wristwatch: a little before 0300. They were running fifteen minutes ahead of schedule.

He carefully slipped the navigation packet from his web belt, and was unfastening its protective plastic cover when they hit the log.

The raft took the brunt of the impact along its right side, and as the partially submerged obstacle slammed against MacArthur and Collins, throwing them from the craft, Chandler felt the packet being jerked from his hands by a crushing wall of water.

The raft twirled around madly, its aft section snagged on the jagged log, and as the water poured in, covering men and equipment, Ross yelled, *"Lifelines!"* Then, "Chad! Matt! Over here!" as he shoved against the log with all his weight, trying to push the craft free—the sharp splinters of wood had not succeeded in tearing through the fabric, but appeared to be caught on the tight rope strapped along the outer edge of the raft.

Chandler and Sewell threw their bodies against the jutting log, and the raft broke free.

"Lifelines!" Ross repeated, and as the raft bounced along the riverbank, the three men locked arms and leaned to one side, pulling on the thin rope attached to their teammates' web belts.

MacArthur and Collins soon appeared halfway across the channel, their heads bobbing wildly in and out of the glowing whitecaps as they fought to swim for the eastern bank. Sewell and Chandler began dragging the rope in.

"The navigation packet?" Ross called out hopefully.

"Overboard," muttered Chandler. "We'll never find it." He glanced up at the sky and strong sheets of warm water showered down, blinding him. Navigating by stars was definitely out, he decided.

"What the fuck—" Cory threw up water as Collins dragged him out of the water and the two men joined the other soaked swimmers. He managed the energy to look around dramatically. "Anybody get the license plate of that submarine?"

"Wasn't no sub, sonny boy," Collins pointed back out at the wild rapids in the middle of the river. "More like an old light pole from somewhere upstream." Most of the log was submerged, but four or five feet jutted up through the surface, pointing directly upstream. "We're lucky to be alive. Saw two damn good men bite the dust back in Recon school when the same thing happened to them. Punched a hole right through one marine's chest. Struck the other in the head, collapsing his skull across one side. When they fished 'em out of the depths of the powerplant dam the next day . . . well, it wasn't a pretty picture."

"I can imagine," Cory said, staring out at the log's outline against the black of the night. The high phosphorus content in the water made the rapids glow in an eerie fashion.

"We better get a move on," Ross cut the lecture short, "if we're going to stay in the game plan."

"And how do you propose we decide on coordinates—flip a coin?" asked Chandler sarcastically. "I told you: that damn river reached out and grabbed my nav case back there."

Ross produced a small article from within his black coveralls. Sealed in plastic, it was another map. "Not as detailed as the one you had," he said, "but it'll get us there." He drew his commando knife from its ankle sheath and quickly unscrewed the metal top-bolt. Inside the handle, a compass came to light. The men smiled back at him in admiration. "Once again, not as fancy as the one you had, but it'll get the job done."

Collins took Ross's knife and examined it. "Shit, they come up with the darndest things back at LZ London."

"It's Saigon-made," Ross corrected him, taking the blade back. "Cheap Charlie's Incorporated, 714 Le Van Duyet."

"I'm impressed," whispered Sewell, and he checked his wristwatch, "but I think we better quit jawing and get a move on."

"Slice up that boat," Ross directed. "And bury it under those vines there. Chad and I will locate a trail if we can. This river is used extensively in the daytime. There's probably a whole network of 'em a few yards up from the bank. Keep your eyes and ears open. This *is* South Vietnam, but few will dispute the Cong control this region after dark."

Ten minutes later, they were heading down through the trees, into the valley directly northwest of Katum.

"Perhaps fate dealt us a lucky blow," Ross whispered as they reached a bend in the narrow trail and lights of a distant encampment came into view, fuzzy and dim along the mist-enshrouded horizon. "I should have plotted our route inland much sooner. Chances are, the Cong got sentries all along the river down there. And probably a whole battalion spread out on the other side of the installation, toward the direction of Saigon. But who would expect an attack from this angle—"

A bullet slammed into the trees beside Ross, splitting the slender trunk of one sapling all the way to the ground. The slap of a distant discharge reached them a second later, and the men all spread out and produced their weapons.

Chandler did not even realize he was moving in a rapid low crawl towards the enemy rifleman. His instincts just seemed to take over after he saw the muzzle flashes fifty yards away. He sent two five-round bursts at the tree line, strange visions of heroism filling his head, and then it hit—a deafening wave of explosions as over two dozen guerillas began to fire at the men scattering for cover behind him. Chandler hugged the earth, keeping his head low, his rifle tucked in at his side.

A low ridge separated himself from the Communists. He was not sure they could see him—but surely they had not missed the muzzle flash when he'd sent the two initial bursts in their direction.

Chandler waited nearly a whole minute until the crescendo of discharges finally began to die down and metallic clicks signalled that the Vietnamese in front of him were slamming fresh clips of ammo into place.

He rolled slightly onto one side and glanced back, looking for his team. They were one with the tree line, but he could still see their distinctive muzzle flashes barking at the darkness. Every fifth or sixth round was a sizzling tracer, and Chandler ducked as a glowing red "volleyball" from Cory's rifle rushed toward him then abruptly arced out beyond the ridge and exploded into a shower of sparks as it ricocheted off a slab of rock.

A dozen green tracers shot back in reply, leaving silver plumes of smoke behind that lingered mere inches above his head. He heard Collins give a crazy war cry, then unleash a full magazine of tracers on automatic. The air overhead became a psychedelic neon ceiling as the chemical-coated bullets zinged back and forth at blinding speed.

Chandler ran his fingers along his ammo pouch. It felt like he had about seven magazines left. That meant something like 200 rounds.

Not enough to get anybody through a genuine firefight.

He decided then and there to lob the last of his grenades and beat a hasty retreat. The team was obviously outgunned. This was no time for heroics.

Chandler yanked the safety pins from two grenades and threw them as hard as he could, then flattened himself against the ground.

Two muffled explosions erupted on the other side of the ridge, but they were barely heard—something as noisy as a locomotive was crashing through the trees in front of him. The air came alive with the grating sound of metal clanking upon metal, and the ground beneath Chandler began to vibrate.

An armored track!

The thought of a Viet tank bearing down on him

sent a sudden shiver down the American's spine. He rolled hard to one side, ignoring the rifle stock as it dug into his stomach and battered his arms.

Seconds later, the NVA T-54 roared across the small stretch of ground he had just been occupying, ripping out a line of shrubs and gouging a wheelbarrel full of black earth aside as it spun to the left and aimed its long cannon at the muzzle flashes coming from the "long-nosed" intruders.

A deafening blast spouted from the barrel the instant the tank rolled to a stop; when the bright flash of the discharge faded, and darkness rushed back over them, Chandler jumped to his feet.

His last two grenades in hand, he sprinted alongside the monstrous hulk of metal and leaped up as high as his leg muscles would propel him.

"Here's one for Big Chad, you fucking cunts!" He kept his left arm wrapped around the hot barrel and rammed the frag into the smoking hole at the end.

Two thoughts raced through his mind just then: that the grenade would rupture the barrel at the halfway point, killing him; and that the tank commander would fire another shell just as his hand was in front of the track's huge muzzle.

Neither thing happened.

A hollow blast from within shook the barrel under his arms, and pieces of shrapnel erupted from the opening, but there were none of the desired screams.

The tank seemed to lurch back slightly as another explosion propelled a heavy shell out at his besieged team members, and Chad decided grenades down the barrel were useless—the vehicle's breech mechanism would protect the men inside from flying shrapnel.

He would have to slide down toward the track and get onto the main body of the tank—use his last frag on one of the hatches. He wasn't sure if he'd be able to get them open or not.

A bullet struck the barrel a couple feet from where he was holding on with both arms, and the round ricocheted an inch from his ear. Chandler was no fool; he knew his luck was about to run out at any moment.

None of his usual A-soldier-gets-to-choose-the-place-and-time-and-manner-of-his-death philosophy clouded Big Chad's mind just then. He was thinking about his fellow soldiers a few yards away. They were under fire—they might even be dead by now— and he had to use this opportunity to save them. That was the only thing on Chandler's mind just then: loyalty to his brother troopers. Honor for himself. Duty to his country's cause, however puzzling. Somehow, perhaps it all came together after all.

Another burst of rounds danced off the barrel a foot from his arms, singing a metallic song for him as they bounced off into the night. A tracer slashed through the humid air in front of his face, leaving that peculiar licorice taste behind. It was still dark, but the sporadic fire from both sides illuminated the scene around the tank in a ghostly blur of silvers, whites, and yellows—and everyone knew a caucasian was hanging on for dear life to the smoking barrel.

"Get the hell out of here, you guys!" he yelled at the top of his lungs, visions of more tanks rolling down from the prison camp filling his head. "This is it! This is fucking it! See you in life numba three, boys!"

No one answered him with words, but a constant eruption of muzzle flashes along the ridge in front of the tank told Chandler his friends were not going to desert him.

A hatch in the center of the tank creaked open, and a skinny weasel of a tank commander—wearing a cumbersome, bug-eyed CVC helmet—popped his head out into the open. "Well fuck my good luck!" Big Chad screamed like a maniac, as he tore the safety pin from the grenade with his teeth and flung it at the shocked Vietnamese.

The Communist ducked, pulling the hatch back down with him, and the grenade bounced off the edge of it and rolled along the ground on the side of the tank.

Chandler brought his legs up and wrapped them around the barrel, hoping it would leave less of him vulnerable to the shrapnel he knew was coming.

The blast nearly caused him to black out, and a stinging sliver of metal tore into the calf of his right leg, but he managed to hang on. He let go with his right hand after the tank fired another shell at his men behind the ridge. Drawing the revolver from his belt holster, he aimed the 7.62 Tokarev at one of the plexiglas shields through which the driver guided his vehicle, but the heavy-caliber rounds merely sent a spiderweb of cracks out from the four points of impact and failed to penetrate.

"Oh, no, you don't!" Chandler laughed, as the barrel began swinging to the left as if to throw him off. The movement was not swift enough to throw him free, however, and as the turret began to stop, he contemplated dropping to the ground and jamming a rock or something in-between the treads, disabling the vehicle—like he had seen in so many of the Korean War movies, but had never actually witnessed while serving in that conflict.

A sharp, stabbing pain shot up through his lower back as the turret began moving to the right again, and it soon spread to his entire body as the Vietnamese thrust the bayonet up into him again.

Chandler yelled his favorite boot camp war cry as a second Communist thrust a three-sided blade into the American's thigh. He whirled around and emptied the rest of the Russian revolver's cylinder, killing the guerillas instantly with head and chest shots.

Then they were all over him on both sides, dragging him off the barrel, slamming him to the ground, kicking his face and sides and groin. Twisting his arms back until one shoulder was jerked from its socket. Jumping up and down on the bayonet wounds in his back.

Chandler began to fall backward into the dark bottomless pit of unconsciousness. He was not sure, but it sounded like somewhere in the distance he was yelling for Ross and the others to forget him, to break and run.

Fourth of July fireworks seemed to be exploding high above him, beyond the space which his fingers could reach out and touch. But they were composed of greys and dull whites and only a deceptive hint of silver.

There was no color anywhere.

Chandler let his head fall back as far as it would go. He felt the freedom of flight coursing through his veins, and then it was as if he were diving backward into a deep lagoon from a high, precarious cliff ledge. As he shot down through the surface, the ripples and waves burst color into all movement around him. The coral along the bottom of the pool exploded with every vibrant color of the rainbow. Brilliant fish the size of puppies floated past before his eyes.

And then Chandler felt himself settle onto the bottom of the lagoon. He felt no need for oxygen, but his chest heaved and the weight of the world came to rest on it. He opened his mouth slowly, frightened now. The bubbles he expected to see swirling to the surface did not appear—only smoke rings of blood, as if suspended in water.

He stared up through the endless sea of water pressing down upon him, and Chandler saw the hungry tigers pacing back and forth along the banks of the jungle lagoon, their green glowing eyes staring down at him. Restless, they waited for him to return to the surface. There was no doubt in the ex-mercenary's mind that they were man-eaters.

He began contemplating the lines crisscrossing the palm of his hand, and wondered if this was the limbo of death between lives.

7.

A muffled cry escaped Ross's lips when the fragment of lead hit his gun arm.

Slammed back into a sturdy *nipa* tree, he clutched the wound and glanced about—none of the others had heard him. The constant roar of automatic weapons fire was too intense.

He sprayed the North Vietnamese tank with the few rounds remaining in his magazine, then ejected the magazine and pulled the last banana clip from the holder around his neck. Still embarrassed he had let out the all-but-inaudible scream when shot—he could never remember it happening before—Ross took the now-empty ammo bandolier and wrapped it tightly around the flesh wound in his right bicep. The bleeding, confronted with direct pressure, quickly subsided despite the frantic thumping of his heart.

A few feet to his left, Collins was firing rapid shots on semi-automatic, moving the barrel slightly from side to side as he directed each individual round at a different target.

On his right, Sewell and MacArthur had also taken

their weapons off full-auto. They leaned their shoulders heavily into *areca* tree trunks, intense looks on their faces. None of the men so much as stole a glance at Ross for directions—even though all four men were running dangerously low on ammunition. They were resigned to the grim fact this was their cemetery; the thought of retreating never entered their minds. Not while one of their own was out there alone, engaging the enemy now in hand-to-hand combat.

"Pull back!" Ross gritted his teeth and gave the unforgivable order.

For the first time, the heads of all three men turned his way. Ross's heart sunk as betrayal flashed in their eyes.

"Pull back!?" the youngest in the team, MacArthur yelled back incredulously, still popping off rounds now at the tank without aiming. Ricochets announced hot lead was still bouncing off cold steel.

"You gotta be fucking us, Roscoe!" Collins roared, ejecting an empty clip and slamming his last magazine into the well of his weapon.

"Big Chad's gonna be the one to get fucked!" Sewell abandoned his usual Me-First attitude.

"You can't leave him out there, Justin!" Cory added. He lobbed a grenade at the soldiers appearing several yards to the right of the tank. Several shattered rifles were thrown airborne by the blast that followed. A booted foot, severed at the calf, landed next to the youth, and he kicked it over the ridge, repulsed.

"Chandler's dead meat!" Ross waved them away

from the low hill rising between them and the Vietnamese soldiers. "And we're running low on ammo! Pull back!"

Chandler's earlier scene on the mountainside flashed through all four men's minds right then, but Ross refused to buckle under to emotion. They could never take out a tank and its support troops—they just did not have enough armament. It would be better to retreat, regroup, resupply, and return to fight another day.

Cory had three magazines left. He fired off his rifle on full-auto, and after the last tracer smoked out across the clearing and shattered against the metal turret clanking toward them, he ejected the spent clip and threw one mag each to Collins and Sewell. He inserted the last clip into his own weapon, then threw his shoulder back into the tree trunk for support and resumed popping off rounds at the guerillas advancing cautiously behind the T-54. "Fuck no, Roscoe! We won't go!"

Collins and Sewell shrugged their shoulders, grinned, and imitated the kid, repeating his chant like green recruits singing cadence behind a drill sergeant back at boot camp. "Fuck no, Roscoe! We won't go!"

Lieutenant Ross gritted his teeth and held in the outburst that was struggling to explode at the outcast enlisted men. He had overdone the pep talks, apparently. OD'ed them on unit pride, team loyalty. Misjudged their rogue mentality royally.

He fought the urge to leave them behind—it was suicide to stay and fight. But he didn't relish putting together another squad of war dogs. Recruiting men of their caliber was the ultimate hassle. He didn't want to go through it again. Not so soon, anyway.

"Shit," he muttered under his breath, pushing his own shoulder against a tree trunk as he prepared to fire off his last shots.

Five more tanks roared up the distant hillside as he pulled the trigger. Looking like purple silhouettes between muzzle flashes, the air became one solid screech of clanking treads as the armor rushed toward the Americans.

It was no use.

All four men fell back away from the ridge, firing as they ran.

A cluster of flares burst above the smoke-laced battlefield as the tanks devoured the distance between the two mismatched teams of warriors. When the Vietnamese saw that the men with zebra faces were retreating—streams of sweat had streaked their charcoal-coated faces—they charged past the tanks, yelling their Asian war cries. Medals were awarded for heads of running-dog foreigners, and there were only four of them out there to be divided amongst the grunts and tank crews.

Ross and his team fired a last few rounds from the hip, then fell into a single-file sprint and disappeared deeper into the trees running along the Song May. They were all seeing visions of their heads being marched through Cong-controlled villages atop long stakes, severed testicles stuffed in their mouths.

"Damn!" Collins clamped his hand over his cheek after the thorns tore an inch of skin away. But he did not protest Ross's decision to leave the trail and head through the tangled trees.

"Jesus!" Cory called out under his breath after the same branch that had caught Brent slapped back in his face too. He moved it aside, ignoring the thorns that bit into his fingers as he kept the way open for Sewell. "Can't we break out the machetes?"

Ross didn't answer, but his silence was response enough: hacking at the trees would create too much noise, offsetting any benefit abandoning the trail had afforded them. The army lieutenant feared the Vietnamese would radio ahead; an ambush could be waiting for them at any turn. But even worse was the well-known fact that traversing any trail in Vietnam after dark—especially at this blind speed—was suicide. Their path would be an obstacle course filled with booby traps. Better to endure the thorns and dangling snakes than lose the family jewels to a jumping land mine. Ross had once seen an infantry-man catch a spring-loaded board full of sabres across the belly. He didn't want to risk that fate either. Before leaving the trail for the trees, they had already come up across two pits filled with bristling, feces-coated punji stakes.

For an hour they clawed their way through the jungle, sweat pouring from their pores, blood covering their clothes from the countless scrapes and scratches. Once they paused while the front half of a huge python—its body nearly a foot in diameter, the scales slick and golden as it slithered slowly past—suddenly blocked their path through the dense trees. But as the sounds of the pursuing platoon grew louder, they jumped over the serpent and pushed on, muscles on the verge of exhaustion.

Ross tried to keep them heading north by northwest, using the roar of the Song May a football field to their left as guidance. The river was normally shallow, but monsoon rains had swollen it to wider proportions until it had overflown its banks at most curves. The ground beneath their feet was soggy and infested with bloodsucking leeches. Ross could feel them clinging to both legs as they sloshed through the shoulder-high reeds, but for now they were only an irritant. It was when they would make it up to his crotch that he would grow nauseous and have to remove them. *And he had thought he'd seen his last leech patrol!*

Another half-hour, and the racket that was a heavily-equipped ground force charging through the jungle began to fade behind them. They hadn't heard the numbing sound of tank treads for quite a while, and Ross knew the T-54s had gone back to the installation, unable to negotiate the soggy terrain close to the riverbanks.

"Can we take five?" Sewell asked Ross as they cleared another hilltop and started into a mist-cloaked valley.

"No breaks until we separate ourselves from the Viets by another klick," Ross shook his head, chest heaving like the others but boots still charging forth, one in front of the other. "We're not out of the kill zone yet."

"But—"

"No *buts*," Ross cut him off, bringing his arm up to shield his face from another thorn-laced branch.

"But I got a fuckin' leech puttin' the tight squeeze

on one of my goddamned *nuts,* lieutenant!" Sewell reached forward and grabbed Ross's wrist.

Ross did not frown. He did not tense up at the physical contact. The coals in his bullet-grey eyes failed to glow. His feet simply stopped moving and he dropped back onto his haunches, relieved a legitimate reason had arisen for them to halt the speed march. "Brent," he said to the team sniper. "Break out the bug juice and help Matt. No cigarettes—the dinks'll spot the glow a mile away."

"Right." Collins kept his weapon slung over his shoulder as he went down on one knee and searched his belt pouch for the small plastic vial.

"Cory," Ross continued, "fall back a few meters in the direction we just came from. You're now an LP. Keep your eyes and ears open. We shouldn't be here that long."

"Roger." MacArthur faded down into the gloom, his steps guided by the dull phosphorescence that glowed green along the rotting jungle floor. A one-man listening post: The directive came as a challenge, and he grinned, forgetting the close call with death the team had just had.

Moments later he was rushing back to rejoin the other men, terror in his eyes.

"What is it?" Ross went down instantly into a crouch. Collins and Sewell rolled away from him, taking cover behind separate tree trunks.

There was anger in Ross's eyes. MacArthur should not have abandoned his LP. At least not under normal circumstances—he should have signaled them by blasting away at the enemy with his rifle. But perhaps these were not normal circumstances:

they had no radio any longer (it was at the bottom of the Song May River with the rest of their gear), and each man was down to his last dozen rounds.

"There's something *big* out there!" Cory was out of breath, blood from thorn slashes coating his forehead and collecting in his thick brows. His teeth flashed against the black backdrop with the rush of words.

"Whatta ya mean, something 'big'?" Sewell had finally gotten his pants back up but was still busy clamping the web belt in place.

"Something . . . inhuman!"

Ross was about to reach forward and grab the kid by the shoulders, shake him up and down—this was no time for riddles and games. But a loud crashing through the trees erupted several yards away, and before any of them could move, a huge Bengal tiger appeared in the air between two sturdy *nipa* trunks. The sleek cat glided over them, surprise registering briefly in its eyes when it finally noticed the men hugging the jungle floor. But it was gone that fast, landing silently several feet behind Ross and his team, then continuing in a mad zigzag rush through the maze of trees.

"Christ!" Sewell gasped, but hardly had the team time to recover when it became clearly evident what had spooked the predator. The ground beneath them was suddenly trembling violently.

Trumpeting loudly for the first time, a herd of elephants—rudely awakened by the advancing foot soldiers—burst forth from the tree line, stampeding straight for the Americans on the hilltop.

"Dig in!" Ross warned, the towering rogues only a

few yards away now.

Sewell, the corners of his mouth drawn back in an insane laugh by the insanity of the moment, yelled, "Incoming!" and hugged a wide tree trunk on the opposite side of the charge.

Instead of wasting time clawing at the ground with their fingers, the others—including Ross—imitated his every move, rising on their toes instinctively in the mistaken belief it made their bodies thinner and less of a target for the startled, ivory-tusked behemoths.

Fifteen seconds later, it was over.

The hill was missing half the trees that had been there at sunset. Dust of the rotting vegetation lingered in the air, making Sewell sneeze.

In the distance, the angry herd could still be heard screaming at the night with their nasal trumpets—but the racket was slowly fading.

"Now that's what I call *close!*" Collins wiped dust from his clothes and promptly slipped in a pile of dung. He fell unceremoniously onto his buttocks.

A tracer round flashed through the space his body had just been occupying and smacked into a tree, the arc of red light suspended in the air before them one second, then gone—like a futuristic laser-beam blast—the next.

"We got *trouble!*" Cory yelled as he whirled around and fired three shots at the squad of soldiers charging toward them out of the tree line.

"Frags!" Ross called out over the exchange of hot lead. "If you got 'em, light the bastards up!"

Without further conversation, the men threw what few grenades they had left, then began moving backward away from the enemy. They traded off when it came to remaining behind the others for a few seconds to lay cover fire—first Collins, then Sewell, then Ross.

"That's it! I'm empty, Justin!" Cory called over to the lieutenant. Ross drew his pistol and threw it to the kid, then placed some carefully aimed shots at the closest Vietnamese's beltline, hoping for a lucky hit on a frag or RPG. The jungle held no such luck that night.

"Make your way down to the river!" he directed. "We'll have to swim for it!"

"Which way is the *right* way?" Cory was totally confused now—they had dove and rolled and somersaulted around so much in the last five minutes he had lost all sense of direction.

"Run for the sound!" Ross reached out and whirled MacArthur to the left, pointing him at the Song May. The string of discharges from the Vietnamese guns tapered down, and he could suddenly hear the splash of the rapids.

"Now move!" Ross urged him forward, and after popping off two more rounds at the war cries erupting along the black tree line, he bolted down the hill, struggling to catch up with the others.

At the bottom, the land flattened out and the trees became less dense. They could actually sprint now, the glow of rotting vegetation all around providing enough light to guide them through the jutting obstacles that often appeared protruding up through the earth's surface without warning.

The roar of the river was all-encompassing now, and the mist in the air almost took Ross back to those camp-outs alongside the Arkansas, back in Colorado, when mountain lions could be seen atop snow-covered peaks, screaming up at the moon. But then a rifle shot sliced through the tropical haze, inches from his ear, shattering the flashback, and he poured what little energy he had left into his pumping leg muscles. "When you get to the bank, *jump!*" The coaching was unnecessary. The men were grasping for those last threads of survival—they knew what to do. "We'll regroup on the other side at dawn!" He used pidgin Spanish, aware it would be confusing enough as it was—the men's frantic thoughts would refuse to shift from English under such stress.

"Something's wrong here, Justin!" Cory skidded to a halt as the roar of the rapids increased dramatically, making the river sound only a few yards away. "Something's terrible wrong here!"

Ross also felt the wave of caution flood his senses. His feet came to a halt and his arms instinctively came out, trying to touch something in the dark. The sensation was like walking through a pitch-black room and hesitating when your nose comes to within inches of a wall. But Ross's men had been running as fast as they could. The sensation seemed multiplied tenfold, striking them harder—almost like a mental force field.

Ross didn't pause to contemplate the phenomenon. He jerked a small flashlight from his belt and held it out in front of him. The beam shot forth a few yards, but faded against the more powerful backdrop of black. There was no river. Yet the roar was so loud—and the mist settling on their lips was definitely no illusion. Sewell held his hand out before him, dreamlike, slowly waving it from side to side as if he were stumbling through a dark room searching for the light switch.

They slowly moved forward together, almost comically . . . one foot at a time, until the sensation intensified, and finally became identifiable: it was the fear of heights . . . that shudder that goes through some people when they're on the top rung of a high ladder, or sitting on the edge of a roof. *Or gazing down at San Francisco Bay from the middle of the Golden Gate Bridge,* Ross thought to himself.

"Jesus," muttered Collins as they reached the edge of the high cliff. Below, nothing but darkness. Ross shined the flashlight down, but it would penetrate the black void only so far.

They could hear the river a thousand yards below, but couldn't see it.

"To think I almost took a running dive," Collins sighed, sitting back on his haunches.

Sewell was glancing back in the direction of the Vietnamese soldiers. "What the fuck we gonna do now, Ross?"

"Somebody gimme a pocket flare," the lieutenant replied. "Make it snappy."

Cory threw a large rock over the edge, but they could not hear a splash—the rapids were too loud.

"I don't have any goddamned pocket flares!" Sewell grumbled, angry his life was coming to an end in this manner. *A genuine cliffhanger,* he complained to himself, *And nobody around to even film it for posterity.*

"I don't have any, either!" Collins ran his hands

over his pockets and jerked open the covers of all his ammo pouches. "I don't even know why I'm looking for them."

"*You're* the only one who ever carries the damn things!" Cory reminded the lieutenant, and Ross frowned, glanced down at the flashlight sadly as if they were about to part under regrettable circumstances, then dropped it over the edge.

The end opposite the bulb was heaviest, so they were able to follow the trajectory of the flashlight as it fell toward the river.

For several seconds it just continued to grow smaller and smaller, threatening to disappear without bouncing off anything, then—just as the pinhead of light was almost gone—it ricocheted off the sharp rocks below, briefly illuminating some waves before vanishing in a distant shower of sparks.

"Fuck me," Sewell uttered the words so that his meaning was clear to the others: *No way I'm jumpin' into that!*

"Must be half a mile down!" Collins held onto Cory as he leaned over the cliff's edge slightly. "We never passed through a gorge like this on our way down from Cambodia!"

"We're back in Cambodia right now," Ross advised him.

"But we never came down through this section of white water, Roscoe," Collins maintained. "I'd of remembered a canyon this tall."

"Maybe it forked upstream somewhere," Sewell suggested. "It's dark—it was dark when we left the Khmer camp. We just never noticed. . . ."

I noticed, Ross thought to himself, remembering

the eerie feeling he had gotten as they'd paddled through the gorge. He had known at the time high cliffs were rising on either side of them, but it just hadn't seemed important. So he hadn't even mentioned it. What would it have mattered—he'd never thought they'd be back this way. And when they *did* return, the race through the trees had left him almost as disoriented as the others—he never dreamed they could cover so much ground in so little time. He thought the gorge would be another mile or two upstream.

"It's been nice knowing you guys." Cory clutched the Indian medicine man's pouch he had worn around his neck through every mission since they had left LZ London. "See you in the hereafter," he said, starting toward the edge of the cliff. "Wish you could fly like me. . . ."

Ross glanced back at the tree line. The Vietnamese would be upon them any moment. Already he could hear the metallic clangs and harsh grating noises that signaled bayonets were being slapped into place.

He glanced back at the pit of darkness stretching out in front of Cory, then his eyes raced toward the tree line again. Indecision flooded his mind, and for the first time in his life, Justin Ross was unable to move his feet.

But his hand darted into a tiny pocket sewn inside his collar, and he pulled out the sealed packet containing the cyanide capsule.

His eyes were drawn to Collins suddenly. The burly ex-policeman had been watching him the whole time, waiting for a command.

Ross shuddered, embarrassed despite the dark—

Brent had probably not seen anything—and then he threw the capsule over the edge of the cliff and fell to his knees.

Collins flew down next to him, and together with Sewell, they aimed their precious last rounds at the enemy.

Ross, his chin jerking around involuntarily—as if by a pang of conscience—searched the edge of the high cliff for Cory MacArthur, but the youngest member of the team was nowhere to be seen.

8.

A soaring projectile shot up through the dark sky. Ross glanced back over his shoulder again because it was almost as if the missile had been launched from behind them, instead of by the Vietnamese—and the flare popped a mere hundred feet above the tree line. Swiftly drifting on its torn parachute back to the ground, its flickering yellow light cast long shadows off the soldiers charging the Americans, making them look deformed and tall as monsters.

"I'll start on the right!" Ross yelled, curious why the enemy troops would launch a flare almost directly over their own position. "Matt, you start on the left! And Brent, you take out as many in the middle as you can!"

"I'm down to my last five rounds, Justin!" Collins lashed back at the lieutenant.

"Then I wanna see *five* Commie heads roll!" Ross was equally as angry. He took in a breath, held it, then slowly squeezed the trigger until the weapon bucked and a charging NVA soldier on the far side of the clearing was catapulted backward off his feet.

"Lucky shot, Roscoe!" Sewell laughed the sort of

helpless chuckle men release when they know they're doomed and there's nothing they can do about it.

"So where's my stuffed teddy?" Ross replied, himself grinning now as he sighted in on another running target.

Collins pulled his trigger five times, and three Vietnamese belly-flopped into the muck, screaming their lives up at the starry night. "That's it, guys!" His tone was apologetic. "My cookie jar's empty."

Ross pulled a commando knife from his calf sheath and handed it over to the ex-marine. "Here!" he said, fully aware Brent had his own blade. "I wanna see some intestines fly before they cancel our tickets!"

"At least I'm not gonna die beneath the tracks of a Russian tank," Sewell whispered under his breath. "That's always been my nightmare. At least they're not gonna crush me into the muck."

As if in a dream, triple arcs of green tracer lashed out a few yards over their heads from behind, rescuing them. The rain of smoking lead tore into the reeds between the Americans and the tree line, snapping the legs out from under a dozen Vietnamese.

Ross and his men nearly broke their necks turning to pin down the source of the shooting. MacArthur's face flashed through the lieutenant's mind, but the youth was still nowhere in sight.

"That way!" Princess Raina appeared on the far side of the gorge behind the tracer light. "There's a footbridge *that way!*" Several Khmers knelt in front of her, smoking rifles against their shoulders, taking aim at the tide of Communists rushing forth from the trees.

Ross was ecstatic: one of the Cambodians popped another flare over the enemy soldiers, and as it drifted along on the warm breeze, he could make out the outline of a swaying footbridge only a hundred or so yards up from their present position. The chasm between the army lieutenant and the princess was about fifty yards across; he wasn't sure they could make it. But hope had entered their dilemma and the rope-laced collection of planks afforded a rare last chance.

The Khmers unleashed another barrage of small arms fire—this time using no tracers.

Ross didn't have to speak; Sewell and Collins both knew the tribesmen on the other side of the gorge were laying down an effective wall of cover fire. Without the tracers, the forms on the far canyon wall again faded into the night—except for their muzzle flashes—and Ross sprinted for the bridge, Sewell and Collins on his heels.

"*Run*, you son of a bitch!" Collins urged the chopper pilot on as the sprint dragged the last reserves of energy out of the man and he began to lag behind. Ross slowed, grabbed the pilot's left arm, and helped Collins pull Sewell back in stride. A few moments later, they reached the bridge.

"Watch your ass!" Ross warned. "I've used these makeshift contraptions before—sometimes the planks tend to crumble under your feet. Keep a sturdy hold on the ropes!"

"Greetings!" Cory popped up in front of them out of the darkness along the bridge's moorings.

"Where the hell did you come from?" Collins

exploded. Sewell, bent over beside him with a sideache, glanced up at the kid and grinned with relief, but kept panting heavily.

"I thought you were history!" Ross yelled as the four of them started across the bridge, MacArthur in the lead.

"I wasn't about to stick around and fight a losing battle," he said, foot slipping between two broken planks. He dropped in front of them like a dead weight and nearly plummeted to the raging waters below, but Collins grabbed his belt from behind and held on.

"I told you to keep hold of those ropes!" Ross yelled again, fighting to be heard above the roar of the rapids a skyscraper below them.

"So I started climbing down the side of the cliff," Cory continued, as if there had been no interruption.

"We thought you jumped!" Sewell accused him, pointing a rigid finger.

"I oughta shoot you right now for desertion!" Ross was steaming. "Lucky for you my bullets are too precious due to supply and demand."

"Hurry!" Princess Raina was screaming at them now. They were halfway across the bridge, struggling to negotiate the missing and broken planks. "We booby-trapped this bridge long ago—we are going to torch the det fuse running underneath it now! Hurry!"

Ross glanced back over his shoulder; the Vietnamese were across the clearing now and had started over the bridge. The ones in front had their rifles up to their shoulders.

"Hurry!" he echoed Princess Raina's request as

fear sent his adrenal glands flowing; one round from the carbines could punch air holes through all four of them! "Hurry!"

Two Khmers appeared beside the princess, carrying blazing torches. She nodded her head, and they climbed down to the bridge's rope moorings and rubbed the torches against a leather pouch hidden from view. A flash of white flame erupted in front of them, illuminating the princess in her black calico pantaloons and thick khaki shirt, then the black-powder fuse ignited and began racing beneath the Americans' feet, from the Khmers' side of the bridge to the other. Attached to thermite packets, by the time the fuse reached the far side, the thick ropes supporting the bridge would collapse, and anyone left on the swaying structure would plummet to their deaths.

"Hurry! Please hurry!" the princess called out again, but her request was quite unnecessary: the Americans were running as fast as they could, under the circumstances.

With forty feet to go, Sewell was struck in the back by a small-caliber round and knocked off his feet. Collins and Ross stumbled over him as the fuse reached the far end of the bridge and a muffled explosion sent the structure to swaying wildly from side to side. "Hurry!" several Khmers crowded at the end of the bridge, reaching their arms out to the Americans as the far side tore away from the cliff wall and began falling into the chasm.

Several of the North Vietnamese troops had already started across from their end. They now lost their balance and toppled over the side, screaming in terror as they began the long fall to the sharp rocks below.

Cory had stopped to turn back and help the others, but a daring Khmer raced out across several crackling planks and latched onto his arm. "The others!" MacArthur yelled in protest. "We gotta help the others!"

But the larger Cambodian kept pulling, and the kid was soon dragged onto solid rock beside the princess's feet.

Like a huge bullwhip that had lost its sting, the bridge sprang away from the far wall of rock and collapsed, but the end moored to the tree trunks rising up around the Khmers held tight, and the Americans clung to the planks as the limp structure smashed against the sheer cliff beneath Princess Raina, sprang back like a giant accordion, then settled against the towering walls of limestone and grew still.

Hanging precariously from loose planks and shredded rope, Ross, Collins, and Sewell held onto each other and slowly pulled themselves up as the creaking structure dangled over the deep chasm. Now and then a plank would give way under their feet and flutter free, but the team never lost their grip and refused to give up. The sound of the planks slamming into the rocks below was an incentive for the Americans to hold on.

"How bad is it?" Ross struggled for a better handhold as several Khmers above reached down to them.

"The bastard got me in the fleshy part, lower back," Sewell said. "My ass is soaked in blood, but

I'll make it—no vitals hit."

"You *better* make it!" Ross allowed a grin to curl his lips as a strong young Cambodian grabbed hold of his collar. "You're the only medic I got."

"Eat," Princess Raina slid the platter of rice back in front of Ross.

He pushed it away again, moving closer to the fire yet sliding his head to the side so he could better watch the girls who were treating his chopper pilot with Cambodian first-aid.

"*Eat!*" she said more forcefully this time, replacing the plate an inch in front of his crossed legs.

Ross grunted, folded his arms across his chest, and tried to ignore her. Nagging women! he thought. Never happy unless they're on your back!

"Matthew will be fine," she said. "All he needs is some TLC. And my girls there are providing plenty of that, Justin."

"TLC?" Ross frowned. The last thing he wanted in his chopper pilot's system were exotic chemicals of some sort.

"Tender Loving Care, stupid," she giggled, inserting her hand through his arm and hugging him tightly. "I'm so glad you are all right. I almost cried back there when it looked like you were going to fall to your death."

"I was a little worried about that myself, Your Highness." He was wondering if the Vietnamese would regroup and find a passage across the river where the terrain was not so dangerous.

The camp they were now in was several kilometers

from the border, deep within Cambodian territory, but Ross's eyes darted up to the treetops now and then, seeking out the birds.

So long as the parrots squawked obscenities at each other, they were safe. When the birds fell silent, that meant trouble.

Ross felt her eyes on him and he gave up, staring down into them. *"Kuhn-yom sraw lan aeng,"* she whispered into his ear sensually. Ross knew they were the Cambodian words proclaiming love, and he felt himself blushing.

Someone walked up beside them, and Ross, welcoming the intrusion yet feeling irritation at the same time, looked up to see the young woman who had been so friendly with Chandler the last few weeks.

The girl was wearing a loose sarong that clung to her ankles. Along the top, it was wrapped under her arms and tucked into the valley between her breasts. The skirt was the color of leaves. She bowed her head to Ross, apologizing for the intrusion, then went down on her knees beside the squatting princess and whispered something into her ear.

"She wants to know where the tall one is, Justin. The man they call Big Chad. . . ."

Ross stared down at his boots, refusing to meet the woman's eyes.

"Tell her Big Chad is dead," he finally said quietly, and Princess Raina drew in her breath, shocked over the news. "Tell her the Communists killed him during a fierce battle. Tell her I saw the bayonets plunged into his back myself. . . ." Ross swallowed hard and shifted about in the soft grasses next to the licking flames. Embers popped and cracked and floated away on the hot evening breeze.

"But. . . ." the princess started to protest on behalf of the girl kneeling next to her.

"Tell her he was very brave."

The girl seemed to sense the direction the conversation was turning, and she whispered into the princess's ear again, broke down crying, then rose to her feet and ran away, hiding her face in her hands.

"She says she is with child," the princess translated. Her words were without emotion.

Ross shook his head slightly from side to side and looked away. Around another campfire, several young women were dancing wildly in a circle. Naked from the waist up, their sweat-slick breasts bounced about with each footfall. A number of animal-hide drums were keeping a fast beat, but there was no music. A dozen men hummed a savage tune in rhythm with the drums, but they appeared to be paying more attention to their primitive percussion instruments than any of the beautiful maidens.

"I will submit a report," Ross said after several silent minutes contemplating the dancers. "I will see to it that the U.S. government compensates her."

Suddenly angry, Princess Raina rose to her feet and struck him on the top of the head. Ross hardly felt the blow. "You fool!" she said. "She does not want your greenbacks—she wants her man!"

Swallowing hard, Ross reached out and grabbed her wrist. He started to jerk her back to the ground, but several tribesmen with carbines in their hands and belts of ammo wrapped around their chests rushed up around them.

Princess Raina threw a hand up and rattled off a few calm words in Cambodian, signaling they were to be left alone. The short warriors melted back into the trees silently, and she sat back down beside him.

"I'm sorry," Ross said simply.

"We have had more trouble with the Lu-long clan," she said, choosing to change the subject. "Their new leader vows to wipe us off the earth like dust. I do not think it would be that easy, but I am tired of fighting."

"What can be done to satisfy them . . . to bring peace to this stretch of jungle?"

"It is impossible. They are upset my people obey the government. We grow mangos instead of opium poppies. The Lu-long clan says we are wrong for obeying the lackeys in Phnom Penh. They say we must be driven from this valley and every valley in Cambodia. . . ."

"But you are a princess . . . these are your people," Ross argued quietly.

"Royalty means nothing to the Lu-longs, Justin. And it means nothing to me. It is an accident of birth. We wish only to be children of nature . . . to be left alone in the wilderness."

Ross watched her wipe tiny beads of perspiration from her forehead with a silk scarf. The campfire flames played across her high cheekbones and drew mysterious shadows along her eyebrows. She looked both vulnerable and sophisticated. A human animal, lithe and agile. He wanted to leap upon her and devour her. "I would think the Lu-long clan would be happy you refuse to dabble in the drug trade," he said instead. "I would think that would leave a larger margin of profit for them. . . ."

"They unfortunately do not think in those terms," she told him. "If we do not participate in the smuggling business, they label us government spies and try to kill us. If we keep mules and walk bales of opium west over the frontier, to sell to the Bangkok black-marketeers, we are labeled competitors, and again they try to kill us."

"It is a no-win situation."

"Yes."

Thunder rumbled in the distance. Ross could feel the humid air shifting about them—heavy rainfall was on its way. The unusual cool breeze announced it. He had emerged from their latest encounter with hostile forces relatively unscathed. It was time to soothe the wounds in his soul. Nothing did that better for Ross than a night beneath a shelter with a woman in his arms.

He watched the princess's lips moving, and his eyes fell to her throat then worked their way lower. "And what about this latest mission of yours?" her words finally reached him. He was following the lines of fabric that protruded from her chest and were made taut by the fullness within. The inner curves were smooth, disappearing in dark shadow, and his eyes saw her as if she wore nothing at all.

"I do not want to think about it," he said. "Not tonight." The simple way he looked at her body aroused the princess, and the tips of her breasts began to protrude, creating more sensual shadows in the fabric.

Ross did not want to think about the camp west of Katum, on the other side of the border. He forced the endless visions of Chandler from his mind, and tried not to wonder why his team had walked right into an ambush.

By now—if there were any American prisoners of war being held at the sight—the Communists would be busy rushing them to another location.

And if the camp *was* only an interrogation center, Mr. Y could send the cavalry in if he wished. The Communists were cocky and defiant. The camp would still be there tomorrow.

Ross watched a falling star burn itself out over the horizon. A false light seemed to be glowing where the meteor had died, and he knew this signaled predawn.

The drums had ceased moments earlier, and as the last flames in the campfire disappeared and darkness rushed in upon their little private section of the jungle community, Ross ran his fingers along her chin and moved forward to kiss her.

The princess took his hand and guided it to her breast, and with the other, he slid her sarong free, opening her body to him. The skirt fanned out beneath them, and after quickly shedding his own clothes, he moved against her, relishing her soft skin against his. He moved in slow, circular motions atop her for several minutes, until her head drew back with pleasure; then she guided him into her. Her fingernails dug into his back as he began stroking, gently forcing himself deeper inside her. She felt her haunches being flattened out against the earth with the pressure and it was as if a fire from within were consuming her entire body.

Her head jerked from side to side as he pumped against her, faster . . . harder . . . and they soon grew slick with sweat despite the breeze. She forced her eyes open as their bodies shuddered, but instead of the stars overhead, as she had expected, the princess was staring straight into the bullet-grey orbs of Justin Ross.

She could see her own reflection in the depths of his eyes, and when their passions peaked at the same time, she was troubled to find she was no longer smiling.

Big Chad was dreaming he was a small bird. A parakeet, caged in a box of bamboo bars, deprived of its freedom. The box was suspended from a horizontal pole, and as it swung back and forth, the parakeet got very dizzy. It quickly became sick and depressed. The small bird was unable to sing, for it was a prisoner, and a huge tomcat paced about impatiently beneath its cage, trying to lock eyes with it.

The bamboo box crashed heavily to the ground, and Chandler rolled with the impact, but when his back slammed against the poles, the pain jarred him from his dream and he realized he really wasn't a parakeet after all, because a bird with any brains at all would have flown right out between the gaps in the crooked bamboo bars.

Spittle splashed across his cheek and arm. Old mama-sans with black betel-nut scowls thrust their rakes and brooms through the bars angrily, trying to jab him in the ribs. An old man with a conical straw hat which hid his eyes threw a platter of garbage against the wide bandage wrapped around his torso, and a child not yet in his teens rushed forward and threw his tiny fist through the bars. It bounced off Chandler's jaw, but he barely felt it.

Chandler stared out through the bars and watched the village passing by as the two sturdy Vietcong carried the long pole from which his cage was suspended. Composed primarily of thatch huts and C-ration shacks, gold-and-red South Vietnamese flags hung from the windows, but Chandler knew he was in a Communist-controlled hamlet. The people flew the RVN flag by day, but the gold star of the VC went up after dark.

"Welcome to Katum, California-swine!" said a hamlet official after he'd walked up to Chandler's cage and dumped a bucket of water buffalo dung through the top. Chandler did not move. He stared out at the man, memorizing his face, but he said nothing.

"Keep moving!" another man—behind Chandler —ordered the low-echelon cadre carrying the pole over their shoulders. "Take him down to the *Truth Or Consequences* game show," the unseen official said in Vietnamese. The words *"truth or consequences"* were spoken in English, however, and Chandler cocked his head to one side, curious.

The meaning registered quickly enough, however. It was the Communists' poor attempt at grim humor—an idiom for interrogation cellblock.

Chandler didn't really care what awaited him at the "game show." He was in such pain from the bayonet wounds it was doubtful the Communists could make matters worse. Every time he moved, bolts of intense pain lanced down through his bowels—and he knew that meant probable internal injuries.

They could beat, kick, stab, and jab him all they wanted—Big Chad was positive he would not talk.

The cadre—young men with indifferent expressions, clad in black pajama bottoms and camouflage shirts—carried his cage without complaint through the center of the village, and as the crowds thinned, Chandler was able to concentrate more on his surroundings.

It became quickly evident the lights his team had seen the night before had not been from a military installation at all, but had been this village. He wondered what surprises were waiting on the edge of the crowded community. He knew the Communists were fond of integrating their military bases within civilian housing areas, but so far he had not spotted a single hint of government compounds.

A distant engine drone caught his attention, and as the Air America plane passed through the high clouds overhead, Chandler shaded his eyes from the sun and stared at it, trying hopelessly to convey a mental message to the pilot. (He had heard about such things, but didn't really believe in them; Chandler knew theories in the field of mindpower only worked if you firmly believed in them.)

The single-prop Cessna flew from sight, disappearing into the belly of a black, castlelike cloud looming on the horizon, never once waving its wings in acknowledgment. It did not circle back. He wondered if they had even seen him.

His cage proceeded along the northern edge of the

village, and after passing through a maze of pigpens, the men carrying it started down into what looked like a peaceful pasture. Smooth, rolling hills of green grass descended to a flat, rice-paddy panorama. Or so it seemed.

After carefully making their way down a dry, narrow gully, the two Vietnamese turned to the right and set the cage down. Chandler stared at the structure built into the side of the hill. Even from the village above it was not visible, because the contours of the land hid it perfectly. From below, along the rice-paddy dikes, the structure probably appeared to be just another wall of gnarled trees. Chandler gazed up at the sky, then he surveyed the land all around—he doubted the structure could be seen from the air.

Thick wood pillars supported the thin roofline of brown-painted cement. A dozen feet of dirt ran along the top of the structure. Camouflage netting was everywhere. The structure appeared to be about twenty-five yards long, but there was no telling how far it ran into the earth. There was only one door, along the side nearest him, but Chandler could not even be sure about that. Past the far end there were tons of earth, beyond that were buried concrete hangers with the open ends kept clear of debris. He counted six of them. Inside were the tanks that had charged them last night. Like some monstrous, slumbering bulldogs, they looked more menacing than anything Chandler had ever seen. He found he was holding his breath—for fear breathing alone would wake them . . . set the huge metal tracks rolling toward him. . . .

The door to the structure opened, and two North

Vietnamese officers emerged. Laughing over something they had been discussing, they returned the salutes of the lower echelon guerillas, and one started over toward Chandler's cage.

The other, frowning at the intense sunlight, remained in the shade, watching. Now and then he would cock his head to one side and glance up at the sky, shielding the sun with his hand. When the officer was only a few feet away from the American prisoner, the major standing in the shade ran out into the open, alarm shaping his face, and began yelling a frantic warning.

A few seconds later, two South Vietnamese Air Force jets swooped in low over the village, unleashing their payload of bombs. The five-hundred-pound shells glided a few meters above rooftops at the edge of the community and impacted inside the rice paddies. A mixture of mud and furious fireballs erupted skyward, and the aircraft vanished as quick as they had appeared, leaving dual sonic booms behind them.

Beautiful! Chandler thought, dismissing any danger the bombing run posed to himself. Running so damn hot they overshot their target!

He expected the F-100 Super Sabres to bank around and make another pass, but they roared into a steep climb and vanished in the same thunderheads the Cessna 0-1 had disappeared into.

ARVN artillery shattered the mid-morning silence next. Like some invisible monster marching through the village, craters "walked" down the main roadway, throwing vast puffs of dust and waves of smoking shrapnel into the air. Huts were blown over by the blasts, and an entire longhouse on stilts was destroyed.

Chandler was confident he recognized the incoming shells of the South Vietnamese 155mm towed howitzers. He grabbed the bars of his cage, preparing to shake them as he cheered, but then his eyes met those of the major with his face against the earth, and he sat back down on his haunches.

The artillery barrage ended as swiftly as it had begun, and the two NVA officers were quickly on their feet, running toward him as they summoned additional men to assist them with the cage.

After it was dragged over against the structure, Chandler was transferred to a holding cell. The officers followed him inside, bolting the door behind them, then began walking slow, intimidating circles around him.

The game lasted about ten minutes.

"Sit down," the major ordered him.

"There is no chair," Chandler responded, his raised chin jutting out at them indignantly.

"*Sit!*" the captain screamed into his left ear, and both Vietnamese pounced on him at the same time, knocking him face-down against the cool cement floor.

He was kicked in the side a couple of times—viciously at first, then with less enthusiasm—and the officers resumed walking circles around him. Clad in khakis, they both wore brown pith helmets with red stars in them.

"Your name." The major's tone had shifted to a quiet shade.

Chandler remained silent.

The captain bent to the side as if to pick something up off the ground, and his sandaled foot shot out, smashing against Chandler's jaw.

"Your name." The major said the words as if for the first time.

"I am the man with no name."

Another kick—this time from the opposite direction—knocked him flat again, and Chandler rolled his tongue around in his mouth, moving the loose teeth from side to side. *He hated the taste of blood!* It was for savages and animals.

"Your branch of service."

Chandler curled up into the fetal position, cupping his head in his arms.

The major glanced over at the captain, and both men grinned. This long-nose was not even resisting. The captain walked over to the corner of the cell and picked up a bucket of water. He dropped it on the side of Chandler's face, bucket and all, and the heavy container brought a gasp of pain from the American.

"Enjoy," the major said coldly. "It is the last water you will get for quite some time to come."

Two guards rushed in, grabbed Chandler's wrists from behind, and twisted his arms back. The captain pulled a set of ropes down from a pulley in the ceiling, and after steel manacles were clamped across the wrists, the ropes were attached and he was hoisted roughly off the ground, arms twisted back and up grotesquely now, straining to pop from their sockets.

"Who sent your squad into this region?" the major asked calmly.

"I have certain rights guaranteed me by the Geneva Convention," Chandler started to claim.

"You refuse to identify yourself, sir. You refuse to supply us with your rank and serial number—"

"I have certain rights—" Chandler repeated, as if he was not listening to the officer, but he in turn was interrupted.

"You are not a prisoner of war!" The captain slapped him across the mouth with a leather sap. "Therefore, you *have* no rights!"

"You are a criminal!" the major elaborated.

"Up to no good, no doubt," said the captain, his grin brightening, and he smacked Chandler again, drawing blood.

"Perhaps after a few hours in this position, with his feet off the ground," the major spoke to the captain as if Chandler was not there, "the round-eye will have a change of attitude."

Twelve hours later they cut him down and dragged him off into the bowels of the dreary structure. Rats scampered out of the guards' way as they walked for several minutes down a corridor that ran deep underground. The walls changed from cement to dirt, with support pillars every few yards, and uncovered light bulbs hanging from wire running along the earthen ceiling.

Chandler got the distinct impression he was being led to his grave.

At the end of the corridor, four conex cells came into view. Chandler's eyes became active and alert as they passed the first two: they were empty.

Before he could glance into the last one on the right, the guards propelled him into the cell opposite it and slammed the door shut.

He landed on his face against the steel floor of the converted storage container. The pain brought him to the edge of blacking out. He could feel more blood draining from the edges of his mouth. Chandler groaned, but did not shift onto his back or side—he did not possess the energy.

Dim shafts of light from the ceiling bulbs filtered in through air holes sliced into the conex door, but he did not feel the desire to pull himself up and look out.

The energy would come with time. And somehow he felt they intended on keeping him around for awhile.

There came an inquisitive squealing from the corner of his cell, and Chandler knew they had placed a rat inside with him to keep him company. The sound would normally have repulsed him, sent him scampering to the opposite side of the conex, but he just lay there on his battered floor, unable to move. Uncaring.

The rat was hiding in the corner shadows. He wondered if it was hungry, if it might pounce on him when the light went out, but then he remembered all the stories the P.O.W.s from Korea had told their doctors: the Chinese were fond of leaving the lights on twenty-four hours a day . . . years at a time. It was part of the psychological weapons arsenal the Orientals were so good at.

He hoped the Vietnamese imitated some of Chinese philosophy—though he was well aware true Vietnamese hated the Chinese in the north (they had invaded Vietnam in the past). He was also painfully aware the rat four feet from his head was not offended by his foul body odor. The rodent, up on its hind legs now, was sniffing the air because the scent of blood was rising from the crimson pool collecting around Chandler's face.

"Hey, buddy!" a voice called out to him from across the corridor, several minutes after the guards' footsteps had faded in the distance. "You American?"

Chandler's ears perked curiously, but the rest of his body did not move.

"Hey, buddy!" The harsh whisper was louder this time. "You hurt bad? I can see the trail of blood leading all the way back up the corridor. Tap the walls of your cell twice if you're hurt bad . . . three times if you're okay. . . ."

Chandler hesitated, then pushed out his foot and tapped the wall three times.

"Ah, yes . . . good! Nice to have some company for a change."

A cautious silence seemed to follow. Perhaps the other prisoner was just pausing so he could respond. Maybe the guy was a Communist plant. It seemed strange they would be the only prisoners in such a large installation.

When Chandler didn't say anything, the other man talked on. Chandler could detect no hint of a Russian accent. His fellow tenant sounded young . . . enthusiastic. *There!* There was the sign of an accent: New Yorker. *Brooklyn.* He was even beginning to sound vaguely familiar. Cory's face flashed before his mind's eye for some reason.

"Just the two of us in here," the voice continued, Chandler listening intently. His mind was still clouded from the beating, but thought processes were beginning to fall back into place. "This isn't a P.O.W. camp . . . in case you were wondering. . . ."

Chandler remained silent.

". . . Just an interrogation center . . . for this region. After they drain what they need out of us and feel they can't torture us any more, we'll be sent north somewhere . . . up the trail and over the DMZ. . . ."

Chandler coughed up some blood. The rat squealed again, but remained where it was.

"You sound pretty bad, pal. . . ."

Silence.

"Want me to summon their shitcan excuse for a doctor? He's got good intentions, actually—but he's only a combat medic, not a real doctor, and you can imagine what their training's like up there in Hanoi. . . ."

Chandler pushed his foot out and tapped the cell wall three more times.

The other man was silent for a few thoughtful seconds, then he said, "Okay, pal. Have it your way. But it doesn't pay to be a hero around here. Nobody gives a shit . . . you know? You're not going to impress any of these dinks."

Silence from Chandler's dark cell.

"You Air Force by any chance?" The man's tone was upbeat again, and something clicked in Chandler's memory. "What's your name, anyway?"

Chandler waited a few seconds as he allowed the memories to run their course, then he said, "How you doing, J.P.?"

Total silence from the other cell was the immediate response.

Then, "Big Chad?" The youthful voice sounded hopeful but skeptical.

"Yah. . . ." The word came out as a painful, exhausted gasp.

"Aw, shit. . . ."

"Yah, J.P. . . my sentiments exactly. . . ."

9.

Neatly aligned rows of tall rubber trees extended out from both sides of the highway only to disappear in the thick silver mist. Heavy sheets of rain rocked the double-decker bus as it slowly cruised down the winding road toward Saigon. A Vietnamese youth had been playing a small portable AM radio for several hours, but now the batteries were dead, and the only sound in the hot, crowded bus was that of the noisy windshield wipers.

Justin Ross and what was left of his team sat in the back of the top section. Cory and Brent had their shoulders propped up against each other, sleeping. Sewell was reading a Doc Savage novel he had found on a coffeeshop stand at the border checkpoint. And Ross just stared out the fogged-up window, watching the endless plantations pass by.

He was going to enjoy this meeting with Mr. Y. Ross had a lot of questions that badly needed answers. Heads were gonna roll. *Why had they been ordered in to terminate an American pilot? ... Why had they encountered an ambush instead?* He wanted to be able to stare Mr. Y in the eyes when he asked him what NVA tanks were doing in South Vietnam less than a hundred miles from Saigon. And he badly wanted to ask the elusive Operations Head why his War Dogs lieutenant was getting the distinct impression, as he raced from assignment to assignment and completed mission after mission, that the boys in the Pentagon were trying to set him up.

The orders had arrived the same way the earlier radio frequency message had been delivered: by air drop. Again, a small parcel under a parachute had been thrown from the belly of an Air America plane, and inside new radio frequencies and a date and time for contact. This time there had been no angry ferret to charge out at them. Ross had had five of the Khmer tribesmen encircling the parcel as Cory opened it— their carbines poised to fire at whatever hopped, sprang, or slithered out—but there had been nothing inside but the paper message.

Which did them no good. Ross had been unable to comply with the orders: ever since the raft accident on the Song May River, the team had been without a radio.

So they had waited. For over two weeks.

Not that it had been time spent idly. Princess Raina had seen to it that the Americans were treated as royalty—insomuch as her jungle encampment could provide. Ross had held nightly briefings, pep talks, and PT workouts with his three men—it just wouldn't have done to let them get lax.

And finally the one-prop Cessna had made another pass over the usual clearing. Ross had been ready for it—he had kept a Khmer youth stationed there during the hours of daylight—and when the craft had made its fly-by, the boy had set off a flare and uncovered a camouflaged message spread out across the ground in brightly painted stones: NO COMMO.

The plane had circled around, dropping another chute. The message inside the parcel had directed Ross's team to report to a room at the Miramar Hotel within seventy-two hours.

Ross had quickly scanned the message, and as the plane made its fourth pass, he had given the thumbs-up signal in acknowledgment. The pilot had waved his wings, then shot up through the clouds and disappeared.

The army lieutenant then had waited seventy-two hours *before* leaving the princess's royal company.

"What's with Mother Nature today, anyway?" Sewell said, looking up from his copy of *Fantastic Island* as another clap of thunder rolled down from the clouds and shook the window pane of the bus.

"Mysteries in the Orient never cease to amaze me," the lieutenant replied in a dreamlike tone, and Sewell shook his head in resignation before returning to his book—Ross sounded like he was off in never-never land again.

"Just hope this storm clears before we get to the city," Sewell muttered.

"Welcome to Saigon," Ross replied, and the chopper pilot closed the book and stuffed it down into a thigh pocket. He straightened up in his seat and wiped the fog from the inside of his window.

A block of crumbling, blackened tenements rose up around the narrow road the bus was descending into, but the rocket-scarred panorama quickly gave way to ground-level shops, overflowing with browsers. Despite the rain, motor scooters clogged the streets, and the bus slowed to a crawl.

There appeared to be a power outage—none of the signal lights were working—but traffic policemen were dancing about atop TCP boxes in every other major intersection.

Makeshift tents, huge umbrellas, and colorful tarps began to spread out on the left of the traffic for as far as the eye could see, and Ross knew they were passing the central market. The odor of fish invaded the bus, becoming stronger when several of the passengers opened the windows for fresh air.

"Nuoc-mam!" Collins awoke, pushing young Cory off his shoulder roughly. "Damned if I don't smell fish sauce! We must be back in ole Saigon-town!"

Several of the passengers turned to stare at him—most were smiling at his use of the Vietnamese words, and the false display of enthusiasm that was pasted across his tired face.

"Where are we now?" Cory shifted about in his seat, rubbing his eyes like the typical teenager.

Ross stared out at the temples rising up into the sheets of heavy rain. Monks in yellow robes were walking in small groups from business to business, collecting their daily quota of free rice. Old women dressed entirely in black fluttered around them, holding umbrellas above the heads of the indifferent bonzes. Nobody answered MacArthur, and the bus continued on in silence for several minutes, the driver making quite a production of his racing skills as he wheezed and groaned with each turn of the sluggish steering wheel.

The bus teetered precariously to the side with each turn into another narrow, crowded boulevard, and the language of the road appeared to be honking horns, as irate drivers squealed out of the way only to block the path of other trucks and lorries.

"What street is this?" Cory had his nose pressed against the moist window. Children in the seat in front of him were imitating him and giggling with delight as he shaped his hand into a pistol and squeezed invisible bullets at them. "Nguyen Hue? There's so many flower stalls out there!"

"Le Loi," Collins corrected him. "We seem to be bypassing Tu Do and Nguyen Hue because of the rain."

"Heading straight for the central bus station," Sewell groaned. "That means we're gonna have to hoof it through this storm to the Miramar."

Ross stood up and grabbed the seats on either side to keep his balance. "Let's go," he said.

Without questioning him, the others rose from their seats and began following him down toward the stairwell at the front of the upper level.

"Check those dudes out," Cory said, pausing to stare out the window again. The bus was now passing a park. Two towering statues of soldiers, one behind the other, as if charging through a rice paddy, rose up through the swirling mist. "What are they? Americans, or ARVNs?"

Ross laughed for the first time since they'd left the Khmer encampment. "There's two stories on that," he explained.

The men paused at the stairwell to watch the slender women in their traditional *ao dais* gowns gathering beneath the shelter of huge tamarind trees near the statue as they waited for Bluebird taxis.

"Some say the soldier in front is American, leading the South Vietnamese into battle, but others are a bit more skeptical. Last time we were here some Brit reporter at the Continental was claiming the soldier in front is South Vietnamese. The one in the rear is American, forcing the ARVN into battle with a bayonet in his back. . . ."

None of them laughed, but an ARVN colonel seated beside the stairwell overheard their conversation and erupted into laughter. "*Good* one!" he said, giving the Americans the routine thumbs-up.

Ross started down the stairwell without replying, and the others followed.

"Please stop by the Miramar," he was requesting of the bus driver a few seconds later.

"Number 115 Tu Do Street," Cory added, carefully stepping over the flowing gowns of two Indian women in aisle seats.

"No go *Tu Do*," the driver sounded adamant.

"Yes go Tu Do," Ross smiled. "Just this once."

"No go." The bus driver stared straight ahead, refusing to look up at any of his passengers. A strong gust of wind shook the bus as it turned down another boulevard, heading away from the nightclub district now. Heavy sheets of rain pelted the windows. "Go Central station."

"Okay, okay," Ross let the irritation show through at last. "Just drop us off here."

"No can stop." The driver shook his head from side to side violently. "This *Express* bus. No can stop until get Central!"

MacArthur moved up in front of Ross, drawing his automatic from the shoulder holster inside his shirt. He rammed the pistol against the driver's right ear. "Pull it over, *barf bag!*"

The bus skidded over onto the sidewalk, scattering several pedestrians.

"*Cam on,*" Cory said sarcastically.

Smiling, the Americans filed quickly off the bus, leaving the flabbergasted passengers with their mouths agape. On the way out the door, Ross handed the man several hundred piasters. "*Cam on,*" he repeated his thanks, this time sincerely.

A strong gust of wind and rain swirled in through the open door with their departure, and rather than soak the first ten rows of the bus pondering what to do, the driver pocketed the cash, pulled the lever that slammed the door shut, and swerved back out into traffic, driving past the first traffic cop he saw. After all, this *was* Saigon. It just wasn't worth it.

The door opened before Ross could knock on it. "Gentlemen, *gentlemen!*" said a man in his early thirties wearing wire-rim glasses and who was completely bald, motioning the four Americans into the hotel room. He did not offer to shake hands.

Collins and Sewell glanced at each other apprehensively, then followed an eager-looking MacArthur inside. Ross paused in the doorway, hand near his shoulder holster, and surveyed the brightly lit interior.

The drapes against the far wall were open, as were the sliding bamboo doors leading out onto the third-floor balcony. The rain had slackened somewhat. He could see a few shafts of sunlight descending down through the ominous thunderclouds floating along above tenement rooftops in the distance. The sound of girls frolicking in the swimming pool below carried up to the balcony, and Ross envisioned five or six of the unaccompanied hookers in their sexiest bikinis, tossing a beach ball back and forth as scattered raindrops rippled the pool surface.

Ross glanced at the man who had greeted them again. He looked frail, and was short and skinny. He wore a safari suit, but his forearms were bone white and covered with red mosquito bites. He reminded Ross of an archeologist who had spent the last ten years deep in the African rain forest, searching for the lost elephant graveyard. *Could this be Mr. Y?*

Two Vietnamese men sat on the edge of the bed on the right side of the room. They looked mean and were wearing Cholon business suits. Submachine guns were on the blanket between them. Security men, Ross decided.

Beside the balcony archway stood a long desk, and behind the desk sat a tall black man with thick eyeglasses, short greying hair, and a beard. He wore a suit also, but had abandoned the sports jacket and now wore his sleeves rolled up. His light-blue shirt was halfway unbuttoned and soaked in sweat. Rain storms in Saigon rarely brought cool weather with them. Only hot, sticky humidity, and clouds of mosquitoes.

"Pleased to meet you! Pleased to meet you!" the man behind the desk said as he stood up, leaned forward, and offered his hand in greeting. His smile was ear to ear and seemed genuine. Cory glanced back at Collins, taken aback, but quickly shook the man's hand. Ross couldn't help but think the face with all the bright teeth looked familiar. A famous politician from the states perhaps? No. . . . Then he remembered: the smile was identical to the billboard advertisements across Saigon a toothpaste company had put up. They had used a smiling black man in the ads, which, to Ross, seemed unusual in Asia.

He started into the room finally, and saw a tall Oriental standing in a corner, a grim look on his face, arms folded across his chest. On either side of him squatted a heavily armed *canh-sat*. Ross couldn't shake the feeling the VNP policemen were the Grim Reaper's bodyguards.

He glanced around the room a second time. Besides the black and the archeologist, it appeared there were no other Americans present.

"You must be Mr. Marsh," the man behind the desk said, staring past Collins and Sewell to Ross, whose cover name was Marsh.

He stopped six feet in front of the desk and made no move to shake hands. "Where is Mr. Y?" His tone was one hundred percent business.

The black man's smile faded, and he sat back down. He got the distinct impression that the army lieutenant in civilian clothes was upset at being summoned to Saigon.

"I am representing the Pentagon," the frail man with the glasses spoke up. "Y is . . . burdened with other matters," he swallowed and shifted his eyes from Ross's. "In Bangkok. He was unable to make it here today. He sends his apologies. . . ."

Ross did not reply to the news.

"So what's the mission?" young Cory said, breaking the uneasy silence with his usual boyish enthusiasm. Collins shot him a nasty look, and the kid got the message. Overreacting, he sucked his lips in as if to keep from saying anything else.

"Your name?" Sewell frowned at the archeologist. The guy reminded him of a biology teacher in high school who had gotten him suspended for fighting.

"Rollins." The man pushed the glasses back up on his nose, but they slid right down again. "Franklin T. I work for the Company. . . ." The look on his face said *that* was explanation enough.

"You mean the Agency?" Collins asked.

"No," the archeologist frowned this time. "The *Company*."

Collins and Sewell both shot Ross a quizzical look. The Company? their eyes seemed to ask.

"Don't matter who he *says* he's with," Ross muttered to his men. He turned back to face Rollins. "Show me your case."

Rollins's frown deepened, but he shrugged his shoulders and brought a hand back to his rear pocket. Ross's fist shot to the gun butt under his shirt.

"Slowly," Sewell cautioned, ignoring the four submachine guns among the other men who had been waiting in the room. The War Dogs were heavily outgunned.

Rollins hesitated, raised his left hand in the air as if surrendering, then with the other pulled out the small black plastic case containing his ID. He tossed it to Ross, who caught it with one hand without taking his eyes off the small man.

Ross raised the document to eye level so he could read it without missing any movement in the background, either hostile or innocent. After a few seconds, he folded it shut and handed it back to Rollins, apparently satisfied. He did not explain to his men who "the Company" was.

"What's the mission?" he repeated Cory's words.

The smile returned to Rollins's face. "I'm sure you know Congressman Stubbs," he said, gesturing to the black man behind the desk. *Of course,* Ross thought to himself. That's where he had seen the man before: in some newspaper or magazine article somewhere. He was a hawk when it came to defense and the military. Ross dismissed his ignorance of politics by telling himself he had been in the jungle too long.

"Of course. . . ." Ross moved forward and held out his hand.

"As you know, the congressman is chairing the House committee investigating narcotics abuse back in the states," Rollins explained slowly. "The committee is looking into allegations a large amount of opium is making its way to our soldiers in South Vietnam and our students back in the states from a segment of jungle in the vicinity you just left, Lieutenant Ross. . . ."

"I see," Ross said, seeming to reflect on the misty valleys that had been home the last several weeks.

"Information has reached us that there is one particular band of hoodlums who are responsible for a large percentage of these illegal drugs coming down from Cambodia," the congressman took over the conversation. "Their leader is a crafty son of a bitch named Lu-long...."

"I see...." Ross said again, contemplating the interesting news. His mind rolled back to watch Collins taking aim on the bandit leader with his sniper rifle. After the vision depicted the round decapitating Lu-long, and after he recalled the smile on Princess Raina's face when his War Dogs had presented her people with the kingpin's mangled head, he glanced over at the Asian standing silently in the corner.

"Meet Mr. Tri," Stubbs said. "He has just completed a lengthy course at the Drug Enforcement Administration." Both Ross and the congressman nodded at the man standing in the corner, and for the first time he produced a bright, bashful smile. "He is a graduate of Berkeley," Stubbs said proudly, "but now it is time for him to return to his people along the Viet-Cambodian border."

"We feel Mr. Tri can bring the feuding clans in the region together," Rollins explained. "With his extensive knowledge of agriculture, he could shift their efforts from producing the large opium crop to products less harmful to American interests."

"Yet producing a similar if not better profit at the market," Tri himself spoke in fluent English.

"This is an experiment better left to unconventional forces," Rollins said as he pushed his glasses back up his nose again and wiped perspiration from his forehead with a white silk handkerchief. "It will be the responsibility of your squad, Lieutenant Ross, to escort Tri safely back into Cambodia, terminate this Lu-long character, and—in your usual crafty manner—insert Tri into the clan hierarchy somehow. He's already well known and well liked, but he's been absent from the jungle scene for quite some time. Many people will be suspicious."

"But with Lu-long out of the picture," Tri said, enthusiasm cracking in his voice, "I *know* I could bring my people back to the right path. They are not that interested in morality . . . what the drugs do to American school children an ocean away. But *profits* they understand. All they really want is a peaceful life in the jungle—away from the cities. They hate making the burro caravans down to the border black markets. Civilized men frighten them. I saw one of the elders die from a heart attack when a car honked at him ten years ago. My people hate the cities. They only want to be left at peace in the mountains and the rain forests. It will be easy to show them how to make a legal income so they can raise *their* children without harrassment from the authorities in Phnom Penh."

Ross nodded his head in mock admiration: it had been a good speech. But for some reason, the team leader was not convinced. He stared at Congressman Stubbs. Ross didn't like politicians. Not even the hawks, who had voted the military big bucks but usually seemed to have personal gain at stake somewhere down the line. He decided not to tell them Lu-long was already dead, his ghost flying circles over the dark stretch of jungle where he had lost his head. Ross always liked to keep a few secrets up his sleeve. The brass didn't have to know everything.

"All right," he said. "I'm one man short, but I think the four of us can handle what you've got in mind...."

"Chandler," Rollins said softly.

"Yes," Ross confirmed. "Was torn in half by a bouncing betty while we were trying to make our way across an abandoned mine field."

"I'm sorry," Stubbs bowed his head.

"We all are," Cory added somberly. He was catching on quickly to the rules of the game.

Ross stared at the frail-looking man with the wire-rim glasses. How did *he* know Chandler was the missing member?

"I'll cable Washington in the morning," the archeologist said softly, "and arrange for full military honors and a plot at Arlington...."

"That won't be necessary," Sewell said.

"We buried him where he was most at home." Collins lowered his head. "The jungle."

Ross released an inner sigh. If Rollins was really Mr. Y, as the lieutenant had earlier suspected, he would never have made mention of Arlington *or* full military honors. Y knew that the War Dogs didn't exist as far as the government was concerned. They were in no way part of the U.S. Armed Forces—officially. Perhaps this Rollins character was just a low-echelon member of Puzzle Palace who didn't really know *everything* about Ross's team or its purpose. Something told him he would have all the answers he wanted very shortly, however.

"Well, I'm sure we can at least arrange something nice for his family," Rollins said, making a last effort.

Ross thought back to when he had first recruited Big Chad into the squad.

He had met him at the airport in New York—after the authorities in Rhodesia had deported him for bungling a cross-border raid into Mozambique to rob a Communist bank. At first, Chandler had not willingly cooperated with Ross while the two men talked in that small Customs cubicle at La Guardia.

But then Ross had shown him the documents. Evidence that Ross's people knew all about Chandler's successful scam to defraud his life insurance company of several thousand dollars—six figures worth, in fact. Proof that Big Chad's wife thought he was dead—victim of a fiery car crash. And after Ross had wondered aloud whose corpse Chandler had placed in the automobile before setting it aflame and pushing it over a cliff, the soldier of *mis*fortune had gritted his teeth and signed the contract sentencing him to life with the War Dogs.

"Yes," Congressman Stubbs agreed, "I'm sure we can come up with some sort of monetary award as an expression of our gratitude for a job well done. . . ."

Ross thought back to the sad scene deep in the Cambodian rain forest, when the young woman Chandler had been sleeping with had told Princess Raina she was carrying the dead man's child. A smile flashed across Ross's face and his attitude turned jovial. "Speaking of compassion," he said, draping his arm around the congressman's shoulder, "there's something I've been wanting to talk to you about. . . ."

10.

Chandler dared not lose his balance by leaning forward. He knew he was sitting on the edge of the cloud. If he leaned forward, he would tumble right off, plummeting face-first into the jagged treetops thousands of feet below. But at the same time, the lush green panorama spreading out below him looked peaceful . . . seemed to be beckoning him, and the bolts of pain demanded he open his eyes. Otherwise, like some drunk driver trying to touch his nose for a traffic cop, he'd be sure to lose his balance.

Sighing in helpless resignation, Big Chad commanded the swollen eyelids to open. The pain increased, like ocean waves at high tide. The wall several feet in front of his face was without decorations—a hazy blur. There were no clouds anywhere around. And he was not floating high above his troubles, after all.

Suddenly the huge fist appeared again. His instincts told him to shield his face, but when he tried to move his arms, he remembered they were still bound behind him. As if in slow motion, the fist started toward him.

The impact itself was far from dreamlike. Knuckles slammed roughly against flesh, and he felt himself falling backward, down into the bottomless pit again. Black spots began to cloud his vision. He felt his head collapse across his chest.

"Wake him!" the major commanded. "Quickly!"

The Vietnamese captain threw another bucket of water in Chandler's face, and, purely out of reflex, his head jerked back up.

The major slugged him again.

"Answer his questions, fool!" the captain demanded, no compassion whatsoever in his voice—only impatience.

Chandler thought back to the time he spent in that Rhodesian cellblock. The interrogator there had been much rougher than these two. And still they had gotten nothing out of him. But now his will seemed to be weakening. His gut instinct was telling him to talk—otherwise he might not survive this time. And survival was the name of the game.

Justin Ross had been impressed with the B.S.A.P. report. Especially when the African police officials had told him about Big Chad's phenomenal ability to resist torture. And when the lieutenant had told *him* about the glowing report—over a beer in a Saigon bar after they'd offed June Wanda—it had made Chandler proud. At least he had some skills. At least he had succeeded at something in his life.

"Talk!" the captain demanded loudly.

The major mumbled some words softly in Vietnamese. Chandler's mind was sluggish, but the translation slowly came to him: *Forget it. We can't*

The captain nodded his head, reached up for the pulley above the American, and released the ropes. Chandler fell to the ground, a groaning heap of flesh flattened out against the cool cement. The major kicked the last bucket of water over in his direction.

Chandler forced his right eye open, and he watched the small pool of water rushing toward him, but just as it was about to reach his lips the guards hoisted his ankles up off the ground, and began dragging him back down the corridor to his cell.

"You will talk," the captain muttered confidently, for Chandler's benefit. "When *The Claw* comes to visit you . . . you shall talk—I guarantee it!"

"Big Chad!" The whisper swirled about his ear and slid into his brain like a roller coaster full of rowdy cheerleaders.

Chandler opened his good eye and stared up at the light bulb in the corridor outside his cell. He was unsure what time of day or night it was. "Hey, Big Chad!" the whisper drifted across the corridor again. "My pretty hallway's lined with blood again . . . you okay, brother?"

Chandler forced his lips into a grin. He pushed his foot out and tapped the metal wall of the conex three times.

"Good!" Air Force Lieutenant Jonathan Pruitt raised his voice slightly. "The way they tossed you into that cell, I was afraid you were dead meat!"

Chandler forced his jaws apart slowly. "They're saving me for The Claw," he said, each word so slow the fighter pilot across the corridor knew he was in saving me for The Claw," he said, each word so slow the fighter pilot across the corridor knew he was in intense pain. "Tell me, J.P. . . . Who's this Claw fella?"

Pruitt hesitated, thinking he did not want to put any fear into the serviceman. Then he decided a briefing on the installation's interrogator might serve to motivate Big Chad. He knew the ex-mercenary would not be impressed. If they could both make light of *The Claw*, it might help.

"They've been threatening to use him on me, too, Chad. Supposed to be an East German or something. Travels from camp to camp, interrogating the special cases—the stubborn ones, like you and me. Supposed to be an expert in the latest torture techniques. The hotdogs in Hanoi treat him like a Moscow Party leader. They say he's got a metal claw where his right hand used to be. . . ."

"Wonderful," Chandler sighed inwardly, tired of resisting. Ross didn't pay him enough to put up with this crap. But he wasn't stupid: he *had* to resist. If he cooperated with his captors, it would only be a matter of time before they put a bullet behind his ear.

The longer he held out . . . the longer he lived.

"Can you talk, Big Chad?" Pruitt sounded hopeful . . . impatient. "Or would you rather I left you alone?"

Chandler gave himself a few seconds to just lie there, then he put forth the effort necessary to speak, "Go ahead, buddy. . . ."

"I been dying to find out," the airman tried not to sound *too* curious, though, "just why the hell are you here in this lousy hellhole with me? Last time I saw you in Saigon, you were some kind of importer...."

"Is this place clean?" Chandler found his energy slowly reviving.

"I don't think there's any bugs, but it *is* an interrogation center—they might have somebody eavesdropping right behind the wall there."

Chandler hesitated, then spoke in Spanish. "Do you know a second language?"

Pruitt chuckled, then replied in Spanish. "It was a required course at flight school. Then where do they send me? Thailand!"

Chandler knew that—especially if their captors were monitoring them with a tape recorder—it would not be that difficult to get their conversation translated. There were enough Spanish-speaking countries going Communist these days. But it would take time. And that was what was most important. "I'm in the military also," he revealed.

"I suspected as much," Pruitt did not sound betrayed, but amused.

"I was ... I *am* part of a secret team ... a squad our 'beloved citizens' back home know nothing about...."

"A secret team?"

"An ... assassination unit...."

"A *death squad?*" Pruitt asked incredulously, his voice taking on a hushed tone.

"We were dispatched here to Vietnam to terminate an individual...."

"Kill?"

"Yes." Chandler was beginning to have reservations. Even though he was an air force pilot, Pruitt was reacting to the news the same way he expected a liberal librarian at Berkeley to.

"Who, Chad? A high-ranking politician in the Saigon regime? A Hanoi politburo member?"

"You."

The word was like a huge hand clamped across the pilot's mouth. The two cells fell silent.

Then, after several seconds, "Me, Chad? Why me, for christsake!" The lieutenant had slipped back into English.

"I wish I knew, J.P." Chandler sounded sincere as he continued using Spanish. "I was hoping you could tell me."

"I swear!" Pruitt was sounding worried for the first time since they had met under these conditions. Almost as if he feared the United States government more than his Communist captors. "I swear, Chad! I've got no idea why Uncle Sam would be pissed at me! You can check my file! I'm a company man. I don't even have a single reprimand in my personnel jacket! I'm true-blue—loyal as the girl next door."

"They don't explain these things to us, Jonathan. They just assign us a target, and let loose the leash. We try not to justify what we do. Quick in . . . quick out. No witnesses, no regrets. . . ."

"Except this time . . . the target was somebody you happened to know."

"Except this time." Chandler swallowed hard as memories of the hot tank barrel flashed back at him, "We ran into a counterambush long before we got to the hit zone. I don't know what happened to the others . . . I suppose they're all dead. Right now, I got two bayonet wounds in my back that're ball busters. The fucking dinks sewed me up good, but I think I'm all infected inside."

"Jesus, Chad. . . ."

"Yah. I'm beginning to think Indochina is the asshole of the earth." He forced a slight chuckle. "I'm gonna pay my travel agent a little midnight visit if I ever make it out of here. . . ."

"If you ever make it out of here . . ." Pruitt repeated his last few words slowly, then hesitated. "If *we* ever make it out of here, what are you going to do about your orders to . . . terminate me, my friend?"

"Let's worry about that when . . . *if* the time comes, J.P. Right now, it's time for a little meditation. I'm already face down on the floor with my ass in the air, so I might as well contemplate how I'm gonna handle *The Claw* when he shows up for our little visit. . . ."

"I see we have some Americans in the audience," the woman on center stage said warmly into the microphone. Ross, who had been enjoying himself until then, felt his lips curl into a frown. The last thing he needed was for his table to become the center of attention.

A spotlight from the back of the nightclub sliced down through the dense cigarette smoke and scanned the tables quickly, coming to rest on a group of uniformed soldiers directly in front of the stage. Patrons around them began applauding.

Ross released a sigh of relief. Choosing a table in one of the darker back corners had paid off.

"And what branch of the armed forces do you happen to be with?" she asked. The slender woman was wearing a form-hugging *cheong-sam*, slit along the side from ankle to thigh. Her hair was jet black; it fanned out across her shoulders and dropped to shapely hips. Standing atop black high-heels, she wore the slightest hint of pink lipstick but no other make-up.

"The United States Army, ma'am!" one of the soldiers called up to her. Americans at another table Ross hadn't noticed sent forth a cheer and started clapping.

The woman on the stage smiled, waved at the distant table, then looked back down at the young private. "And what kind of work do you do for Uncle Sam, sir?"

Ross's frown became a tense grin. She sounded just like an interrogator! *but Christ what he'd give to have someone like her torturing him!*

"I'm not a 'sir,' ma'am...." the private replied loudly, basking in the bright spotlight. "I *work* for a living!" Again, several tables burst into lively applause.

"He's a ninety-five-Bravo!" one of the man's fellow privates called out to set the record straight.

"Oh!" The woman seemed both surprised and frightened, but it was obvious she was just feigning fear. "An MP!" She held her wrists out. "You didn't come here to arrest *me*, did you?"

The roar from the audience rose to a deafening

crescendo. "Only if you don't get on with the show and sing us a song!" he threatened good-naturedly.

Several tables began a steady clapping cadence, also calling for a song.

"Okay . . . all right." She bowed her head slightly and brought clasped hands to her face, Thai style. Soft music—a guitar and piano—started up in the background, but the woman waited a few more minutes for the noise of the patrons to die down. "I want to take this opportunity to make a political statement," she said, speaking the words almost sensually into the microphone as the level of the music rose. Somebody in the back of the nightclub booed loudly, but the woman only smiled.

"As you leave Saigon, heading for Tan Son Nhut airport," she continued, "there is a large white monument in the middle of the traffic circle near the intersection you military policemen," she pointed down at the table of MPs, "have notoriously named Checkpoint Six-Alpha. The concrete wall is surrounded by rusting concertina wire, but I want all you guests of my country to know the sincerity of those words does not also tarnish with time." Ross could see the monument she was trying to describe clearly in his mind.

Drum brushes began sliding across a snare, increasing the drama of the music and the moment. "The words on the wall are very simple," the woman's smile faded, and a sparkle on her cheek almost looked like a tear, "but they convey the true feelings of most every Vietnamese in this city: *The noble sacrifice of allied soldiers will never be forgotten.* . . ." The smile returned to her features, but the woman's high cheekbones seemed tense with overpowering emotions.

The introductory frames of music were just a simple set of bars that flowed back and forth on the scale, not resembling any particular song, but now a second guitar joined the first, and the volume increased and the pace accelerated until it filled the nightclub, and every American in the huge room knew the musicians were opening with an upbeat version of Mickey Newbury's *An American Trilogy.* The applause nearly drowned out the guitars. "I just want you to know!" the woman was yelling into the microphone now to be heard—her smile wider than her eyes now as she too became caught up in the excitement, ". . . I just want you all to know that, despite all the protests across South Vietnam lately, despite any unfortunate incidents you men might have experienced in the back alleys of Saigon-town . . . the real citizens . . . the simple folks like me . . . thank you from the bottom of our hearts for coming here to Veeyet-Nam to help us in our time of need!"

The drummer slammed one of his sticks against the largest cymbal, and the woman began singing first in English, then Vietnamese.

The applause went on throughout the song, with half the house rising to their feet toward the end, and the singer from Hue graciously consented to repeat the entire performance. Tears flowing from her eyes, she began the soothing prologue again, and the Americans took their seats. For this one, the nightclub died to a hush. The only noise other than the musical instruments or her voice were a few glasses clinking as the audience saluted the woman beneath the silver spotlights.

"Pretty damned good," Sewell said, then took the last swallow from his glass. His eyes never left the forty-year-old singer in the Chinese-style dress.

"Aw, she's all right. . . ." Cory twisted another cap off a "33" beer bottle and tipped it over.

"Whatta ya mean, 'all right'?" Collins belched loudly, but the sound was covered by the music coming from the amplifiers in every corner of the building. "Just 'all right'?"

"I'd rather be at the Xin Loi," Cory revealed. "Or even that dive back at the Miramar. They got singers there, too!" His grin flew ear to ear. "And they don't wear no *fucking clothes* when they try to seduce the audience!"

"You were due for some culture," Ross muttered, trying to gauge the singer's bra size, but the tailored dress, closed at the throat, made it difficult. He wished she were wearing a low-cut blouse. His fantasies brought the smell of the rain forest to him, and he began thinking about Princess Raina. He wondered where she was tonight, if she was alone beside some smoky campfire, or if she was in the arms of a young tribesman, spread out on the white sands of the lagoon by the waterfall. The vision made him angry, and he curled his fingers into a fist.

"That ain't no ordinary set of 'fucking clothes,'" Sewell corrected MacArthur. "That golden set of threads is a *cheong-sam*, my friend. Show some class." Matt stuck his nose in the air. "It's time you grew to appreciate the finer things in life...."

"He's too used to snuggling up to some Khmer maiden wrapped in a sarong with fish sauce on her breath," Collins laughed.

"Her *cham-song* is silver!" Cory corrected them, pronouncing the type of dress incorrectly on purpose.

"Well, fuck me!" Sewell glanced over his shoulder. Sure enough, the dress now looked more like it was composed of a million glittering diamonds.

The song had changed to a rock melody popular back in the States, and the singer had invited two Americans up on stage to dance with her. Once again, the crowd had taken to applauding.

"It's the stage lights," Ross said quietly.

"What?" Cory was busy downing another bottle of beer.

"It's the multicolored stage lights. They've got silver and gold and red and blue and you-name-it shades of color on a big turntable down in front of the stage lights. It's slowly revolving. Each time it hits a different color, her dress appears to change color, too."

"Leave it to the Vietnamese," Collins said, nodding his head in the affirmative.

"Who gives a fuck?" Cory leaned back in his chair and tipped completely over. He failed to get up, and the others ignored him.

Ross caught movement out the corner of his eye, and he shifted his head toward the dimly lit entrance of the nightclub. A large party of Asians and

Americans was entering the establishment.

"There's the congressman from Massachusetts." Sewell's voice was taking on a slight slur. Ross's eyes narrowed as he recognized the black politician—nearly invisible in the dark except for his ivory-white safari suit—walking beside Mr. Tri. Behind them, Rollins, his studious look intact, led their entourage of bodyguards.

The three War Dogs still in their seats gave involuntary starts as they spotted a radiant woman in a snappy western outfit gliding gracefully across the crowded dance floor between Stubbs and the Vietnamese. Hair the color of caramel—but vibrant, each strand seemingly alive—and eyes large and liquid green as they darted about the room, scanning faces, she almost looked Asian, but not quite . . . not to the War Dogs. . . .

"*Amy!*" Sewell's gasp came out as a harsh whisper that the men on either side of him were thinking, as the Americans at the corner table in the back of the nightclub recognized their favorite team member.

"Don't say anything," Ross told Collins and Sewell, instantly sober. "I'm not sure what she's into, but just lay back and play along. We don't want to blow her cover." Why didn't Rollins warn them? he was wondering. "Roust Cory down there on the floor," he said as an afterthought. "Tell him what's going on."

Rollins's glasses were down on the edge of his nose again, and his beady eyes were staring out over the lenses as he sought out Ross's table. His cautious grimace transformed instantly into a practiced smile when he spotted the stocky team leader at the table farthest from the stage. He spoke something to the congressman, and Stubbs's eyes darted to his right until he also spotted the lieutenant and his men. He altered the course of the entourage, and soon the bodyguards were moving more chairs around the teakwood table.

Collins locked eyes with Amy as the congressman held out her chair. He did not rise with Ross and Sewell, and the frown on his face announced disapproval. Collins despised blacks who were always smiling like they knew some special secret only victims of racial prejudice were privy to. He didn't like seeing Amy in the company of such hypocrites. It soiled her, he felt, and drew her farther away from him.

"Glad you could make it," Ross told the congressman, taking his seat before Stubbs. His eyes remained on the generous swell of flesh beneath Amy's throat. Her dress had a closed collar and long sleeves. He wondered about the scar across her chest. He had authorized the hospital in Japan to bring in a plastic surgeon. Had they corrected the jagged line that ran from her throat to her stomach while treating her for the gunshot wounds she had received on their last mission?

Collins was watching her hands as she ignored the men at the table and began browsing through a menu nobody had ordered from in years. Her arms appeared to be functioning all right, he decided. No paralysis. His mind flashed back to that harrowing street chase a few months before, when she had been leaning out the car window, firing at the vehicle they were chasing, only to have several rounds catch her in the shoulder and jerk her right out the window. Collins would never forget the way her shapely body had bounced along the blacktop after the fall, coming to rest in a ditch, out of sight. They had stayed with the chase, abandoning her. She couldn't have survived the high-speed fall, they had thought at the time. The mission came first.

It appeared now, as she glanced up a couple times to check Ross's expression, that she was cold as ice . . . despite the sensual, taunting smile. She had not forgiven them.

Amy had never written him while she was away. Brent knew Ross probably would not have informed him if she had died from her injuries. Relationships between members of the team were supposed to be impersonal, totally business. Friendships impaired decision-making during tight situations. And it was harder to recover when a dead team member had been close. He wondered if the love they had shared was dead instead.

"I'd like you to meet our interpreter, Candy," Stubbs said, smiling brightly. "You did not get to see her during our last meeting."

Ross appeared most gracious as he reached across the table, took her hand gently, and kissed it. "Ah . . . you are Vietnamese, my dear?"

Amy twisted her hand from his suddenly iron-tight grip and lowered her eyes, giving him an annoyed glare. "I am Eurasian," she said. "My father was French. . . ."

Ross nodded. He had made a good choice when he'd picked her for the team so many lifetimes ago—her Latino features were almost Mayan, which gave her cheekbones an Asiatic flare. Very convincing.

She glanced at Sewell, who had been quiet up till then. He had the first two fingers of his right hand spread wide and poised against his mouth. When their eyes met, he ran his tongue, snakelike, between them. Amy silently kicked him under the table, and Matt recoiled from the pain and commenced scratching his nose instead, as if it were itching. None of the others seemed to notice. Cory was back in his seat between Collins and Sewell, staring straight ahead, past everyone. His eyes were dazed and unblinking . . . zombielike. They brought the first nostalgic half-smile from her, but she willed it away.

"So how are preparations looking?" Congressman Stubbs asked, flashing his gleaming teeth at Ross.

The lieutenant kept his eyes on the woman still singing atop the stage. Her words, in a soothing hill dialect, were of a maiden's love for her dead warrior brave. The tables in front of the stage were silent; the audience seemed spellbound. "We should be ready to move in the morning."

"Excellent . . . excellent." Stubbs turned to face Amy. "Shall I summon the waitress, my dear?"

But Amy was pushing her chair away from the table. "If you'll excuse me for a moment," she said, smiling as if it were time to visit the ladies' room.

"Of course, of course." The congressman helped her out of her seat. "Hurry back now . . . you hear?"

"Wonderful figure," Mr. Tri said, grinning at the

men as she made her way through the tables, shapely bottom swaying with each footfall and bouncing firmly inside the knee-length tight-fitting skirt.

"An exquisite example of the Asian female at her finest," Stubbs said. He began cleaning his smile with a toothpick.

Collins waited a few more seconds, then also excused himself. "I see an old friend at a table over there," he lied, but the congressman didn't even seem to notice him as he stood up.

Brent raced through the tables and intercepted Amy a few feet from the rest rooms. He clamped a hand across her waist and guided her to a dark corner.

"You're *hurting* me," she said.

"You hurt *me*," he countered angrily, "by not writing. Christ, Amy, I thought you were dead!"

She frowned, biting her lower lip, then took his hand and led him outside onto the veranda. "How was I supposed to know where the team was?" Her eyes grew serious. "You guys could've been in Bumfuck Egypt for all I knew—"

"Knock off the profanity, okay?" he snapped. "It makes you sound less like a lady!"

Amy pulled away from him. "Hey, you don't own me, buster!" she said, her voice rising. She glanced around to see if anyone had heard, but they were alone.

"I thought we had something . . . *special*." He moved up close to her again and placed his hands on her shoulders.

"Well we *didn't*." Her eyes were on fire, but something told him she was trying to put them out.

Collins stepped back on his own this time. "So are you fucking niggers these days?" he said, casting his chin back in the direction of the congressman's table. "Political niggers, as a matter of fact?"

"What are you talking about?" She narrowed her eyes at him. "Mr. Y sent me back here from Tokyo. I'm on assignment, you bastard!"

"'Shall I summon the waitress, my dear?'" he imitated Stubbs's voice, complete with accent. "'Hurry back now . . . you hear'?"

"Oh, stuff it, Brent!" she moved to walk away.

"Tell me, honey," he asked, letting his shoulders drop and his jaw bob up and down with each word as if he were a street tough approaching a curbside hooker, "is his cock that much longer than mine?"

Her face contorted as if she were about to cry. "Leave me alone!" She moved to break away again. "Just leave me alone!"

A young Vietnamese couple walked onto the veranda just then, hugging and kissing, ignoring the world around them, and Brent pulled Amy back into the shadows, behind tall potted plants that were against one wall of the rooftop lounge.

"I missed you," he said, forcing his lips against hers. She resisted at first, then wrapped her arms around him, holding tight.

When they finally released each other, he held her away at arm's length and ran his eyes along the top half of her body. "Are you all right? I mean . . . are you. . . ." The words eluded him. He didn't want to mention the words. ". . . Are you . . . okay?"

Amy's eyes fell to the ground and her body seemed

to grow limp in his hands. Tears welled up in her eyes. "I was dead, Brent," she started to sob. "The doctor on that hospital ship told me they had me on the operating table twelve hours. He said they lost me twice. They don't know how I survived the trauma and the long wait before Ross had been able to get me out to sea. They are amazed at my rapid recovery...."

"I'm sorry," Brent's voice cracked, and he lowered his head.

Amy lifted his chin with her fingers, but her own eyes fell when she saw he cared, but not enough to shed tears. "You left me...."

"I had no choice." He could not look at her now.

"You abandoned me face down in a ditch, Brent ... it was so dark. *Nobody came to help me!*"

"Ross wouldn't let us," he said. "The mission...."

"And then you came back." Her voice grew more steady. "You mopped me up and taped me back together. But it was too late...."

"You're *alive*, Amy!"

"But you should have let me die," she said softly, aware now a very special part of her had oozed out into the earth along with all the blood she had lost that night.

"But you're *here*, now. We're together again. It'll be just like it was before ... you'll see...."

"It can never be like it was before," she said sadly, turning to walk away. "I am not the same person, Brent.... The Amy you knew died on an operating table in a hospital ship out in the middle of the South

China Sea...."

She hesitated leaving the cover of the plants as two more figures walked through the archway leading onto the veranda. Beside Ross, hidden briefly in shadow, was the slender man with glasses and no hair: The company man, Rollins.

The two stopped just a few feet away from where Brent and Amy waited behind the flowering leaves. The Vietnamese couple had returned to the dance floor inside, and Ross turned to watch the gunships executing their tight circles just beneath the clouds as they dropped flares along the edge of the city.

"What's going to happen to that air force pilot being held prisoner near the border?" Ross asked. "Lieutenant Pruitt."

Rollins hesitated, then decided he would not be breaching security by talking to this man: Ross's team was about as top secret as the files got. "Your mission failed," he said matter-of-factly. "Pruitt is probably a thousand miles north of here by now. If you had advised us of your decision to abort, we might have been able to send a reactionary team in there to ensure your safe retreat."

"Our radio was destroyed in a river accident," Ross said sarcastically.

"I see...."

"But there's something *I* don't see," the lieutenant continued. "Why did we run into a counterambush?"

"Those things happen, my friend. This *is* a country at war."

"Why were we not warned there were NVA in the

region? And that they had fucking T-54 *tanks!*" He leaned forward nose to nose with Rollins.

"My people were not aware—"

"And what about logistics?" Ross cut him off. "There's no goddamned P.O.W. camp where the radio message said it would be ... the lights we ended up walking toward led to a snake's nest, *my friend:* a Cong-controlled hamlet." He grabbed Rollins by the front of his shirt and lifted him off his feet. "Now I'm beginning to get the feeling somebody back at the Big P is trying to set me up. . . . And I'm getting tired of seeing my people get hurt!"

Amy, overhearing their conversation, swallowed hard as she felt her insides tingle—the lieutenant was talking about *her!* He *did* care, after all.

"I think it's about time I meet Mr. Y face to face," Ross continued. Amy and Collins exchanged surprised looks—they had both been under the impression their leader had met the mystery man long ago ... when Ross had first been recruited. It was becoming clear how wrong they were—about a lot of things.

"I'm afraid that would be quite impossible, Lieutenant."

"Didn't they teach you at The School *nothing* is impossible, Rollins?"

The Company man said nothing as Ross moved him over toward the edge of the balcony. Collins started to move from the shadows in an attempt at refraining him from doing something they'd all regret later, but Amy grabbed his wrist.

"I want to know what's going to be done about

Lieutenant Pruitt," Ross said. "I've done a little checking up on my own time, and I get the impression young J.P. is a buddy of . . . *was* a buddy of Chandler's. I wanna know what's going on here, Rollins. I wanna know who put out the hit on Pruitt. And I wanna know *why*!"

"I'm afraid you don't have the *need* to know." The fragile intelligence operative remained calm and unemotional even as Ross held him out over the street several floors below.

"What's the congressman's stake in all this?"

"You've already been told: he chairs the anti-drug task force. He just wants to see the flow of opium stop here in Southeast Asia before it finds its way to the streets of downtown U.S.A."

"Why do I find that difficult to swallow?" Ross recanted somewhat, lowering Rollins back onto the veranda.

"What you believe or don't believe is *your* problem, Lieutenant," Rollins sensed he had won a temporary reprieve.

"Level with me, mister." Ross released the smaller man, but his tone turned twice as threatening. "I did a background on Lieutenant Pruitt. Why would our government want my people to go into an enemy camp to smoke his ass? Does it have anything to do with his father?"

"Lieutenant Pruitt's father has been a Korean War MIA for the last thirteen years, Ross—"

"But the kid's been searching for him all this time. And I'm getting the uneasy feeling—a little twitch in my gut I always get when I smell a rat—Uncle

Sammy is worried a hero's son is getting too close to the truth. Now level with me, Rollins: am I hot or cold when it comes to solving this riddle we find ourselves confronted with?"

Rollins forged a deep frown and rested his chin in a hand as if faced with a sudden dilemma. His brows furrowed in deep concentration for a moment, then he looked up at Ross. "Lieutenant Pruitt had never gotten any closer to finding his father than you or me," he said somberly. "Sergeant Johnny Pruitt was executed by the North Koreans three days after he was captured at the battle for Camp Starburst."

11.

Big Chad felt no fear, but he couldn't explain the shudder that shot down his spine as the sound grew louder: three sets of heavy boots walking down the corridor toward his cell.

"Time to bend your head down between your legs and kiss your ass goodbye," Lieutenant Pruitt whispered across from his conex. Chandler forced a soft chuckle. That they could laugh about what was soon to befall both of them *had* to be proof they were losing their marbles.

"Been nice knowing you, J.P." Chandler spoke the words as if each one was precious.

"Likewise, Big Chad. Fucking for sure." The air force pilot gripped the sturdy bars welded over the air holes in his sweltering tomb. "If they take you first, do me a favor, pal."

"I can grant you three wishes, J.P.," Chandler said seriously as the footsteps grew louder.

"Okay . . . great! First, promise me you'll go out kicking and biting."

"And punching," Big Chad added.

"They'll have your hands manacled behind your

back," Pruitt reminded him.

"Oh . . . right. . . ."

"Promise me."

"You got it, brother."

"Secondly, spit in the major's face for me, okay? Before they knock you senseless . . . send a sloppy one smack in the motherfucker's eye, okay?"

"You've got one last wish left, J.P."

"*The Claw*, Big Chad. I can tell: the boots sound different today. They got The Claw with 'em this time. . . ."

"Life is a bitch, Lieutenant. . . ."

"Promise me you'll kick that bastard's balls up to his Adam's apple . . . can you grant me that wish? Can you?"

"They'll tear my lungs out for that one, J.P. They'll peel off all my skin, dip me in rubbing alcohol, clamp *my* nuts in a vise-grip, and tear my lungs out. Is that what you want? You'll have to listen to me screaming when they do it. Think you can handle that?"

"You won't scream, Big Chad. I know you won't."

"They'll probably ram a baseball bat up my asshole, goddamned faggots."

"You're going to die anyway, Chad."

"Yah, you're probably right. . . ."

"So you can promise me those three modest wishes, buddy?"

"You can bank on it, J.P. Cross my heart and hope to die, stick a needle in my eye. . . ."

"Yah, they'll probably do that to you, too."

"Let's not give 'em any new ideas," Chandler's voice softened to a whisper. The interrogators had almost traveled the entire length of the corridor.

"Hey Chad. . . ."

"Yah, Jonathan?"

"What if they take me away first?"

"Silence!" The North Vietnamese captain slammed a billy club against Pruitt's fingers and the lieutenant jerked them back, withdrawing into the recesses of his cell. But he did not cower in the corner—he coiled in the shadows, preparing to pounce.

Metal scraped against metal as they unlocked the door to Chandler's conex. A huge caucasian hand rushed in and grabbed the American's ankle. He was roughly dragged out into the hallway, and was promptly kicked several times in the side.

Chandler instinctively shielded his face, forgetting all the promises he had just made Pruitt.

"Meet The Claw," the camp major introduced the tall German to the man on the floor. "Colonel Parker."

"We would tell you *his* name," the Vietnamese captain told the torture specialist, "but we are unable to get anything out of him."

"No information whatsoever?" Parker's eyebrow shot up, intrigued.

"None," the major confirmed.

"Then it appears I have my work cut out for me," the colonel laughed loudly.

Chandler slowly lowered his arms from the defensive as he realized the voice was growing vaguely familiar. When he saw the German's face, memories of a distant midnight meeting beside an African campfire flooded through him. *The Claw* was not such a mystery man after all.

Only a year ago, while Chandler was plotting a cross-border bank heist in Mozambique, Parker had been the gunrunner who had supplied his people with automatic rifles. At *that* time, shortly before Chandler's group had been arrested and deported by the Rhodesian authorities, there had been no reason to suspect the man was a Communist. They had all assumed he was West German. Parker himself had claimed he was ". . . currently without a country," as they'd argued over the high price of the AK-47s. The man's words were still fresh in his mind.

Chandler wondered where he had lost his right hand . . . In which country across the globe had the German survived such a close brush with death? . . . What warrior was responsible for chopping off the limb from which had grown *The Claw?*

Matt Sewell could not suppress the smile as his hands guided the controls to their proper positions, and the new Huey chopper dropped down toward the gaping hole in the triple canopy.

"Need more branches blown out of the way?" Ross asked him as the flapping rotors sent a warm downblast against the treetops below. Asians bristling with combat weapons crowded behind him.

"No sweat, Roscoe!" Sewell flipped the safety plate off the arming panel. "Looking good, *with room to spare!*"

Several of the soldiers from the DEA task force exchanged hesitant looks but said nothing. Collins and MacArthur were hidden behind the dark faces, manning the door-gunner positions.

The helicopter descended down through the layers of tangled branches, sending tree monkeys and startled parrots scattering. The thumping of the rotors sent the mist along the jungle floor swirling away. "Wish we'd had this baby last time we were in this stretch of woods!" Collins called up to the men in front of the craft. He and Cory both had ear-to-ear smiles plastered across their faces.

The Huey's descent slowed considerably as the rain forest seemed to grow up all around it, and Sewell eased the craft into a hover about forty yards off the ground.

"Arming nose ordnance," he smiled over to Justin.

Directly in front of them, three caves appeared midway up a steep cliff wall.

Startled Chinese gang members, awakened by the huge metal hawk, gathered around the mouths of each opening, pointing at the menacing buglike glass plates in front.

"Stupid fucks shoulda found a new hideout when they had the chance," muttered Ross, relieved the opium-smuggling hoodlums were still where his team had last seen them.

A tall stocky tribesman, totally naked, with a slender woman clinging to his hips as she was dragged after him, appeared in the center cave, sporting a carbine.

"Time to waste a doper and make the world a better place to live in," Sewell muttered softly.

"Wait one," Ross raised a hand. "Let him take the first shot. . . ."

"You just don't wanna see me split that chick's

chest down the middle with my blooper," Sewell argued, still grinning though his lips had taken on a demonic curl to them.

"Just hold off a second. . . ."

"That's not usually the way we work," the chopper pilot reminded Ross. "What happened to 'quick in and quick out,' honcho-san?"

The Chinaman was bringing his rifle up to his shoulder.

Sewell's smile faded and his hands grew tense. Small beads of sweat appeared on his forehead. "I don't plan on droppin' another one of these whirlybirds on the ground, Roscoe," he said nervously. "Old Man Y doesn't find it in his heart that often to replace my toys."

A small puff of smoke appeared directly in front of the Chinaman's rifle muzzle, but they couldn't hear the discharge because of the rotors thumping the air overhead.

Sewell's shoulders tensed and his face cringed slightly, expecting the front windows to spiderweb right in front of his eyes. But nothing happened—not even the *ping!* of a ricochet off the skids. The round had fallen short, or had missed them entirely.

"That clown can't hit the side of a quonset hut," Ross laughed.

"Musta had his bullets made in Saigon," one of the troopers behind the pilot whispered to the man next to him in English.

"Let him have it with both barrels," Ross finally gave the order.

A dozen more men had rushed up to the openings in the limestone cliff when the dual XM-21 mini-guns sent their first burst of 7.62 rounds at 6,000 per minute. A cloud of dust appeared in front of the caves as the bullets tore up the limestone in their travels from opening to opening.

Sewell shut down the machine guns and fired the 40mm cannon in the nose of the chopper. The craft bucked slightly as the projectile was launched by the tap of a fingertip, and an explosion deep in the recesses of the middle cave threw silver smoke and shredded bodies out in a billowing cloud.

"Bull's-eye!" Ross clapped Sewell on the back. The pilot sent two rocket pods full of 2.5-inch ordnance roaring from the right side of the craft, and a rolling haze of smoke and debris obscured the entire cliff wall as the cave on the right totally collapsed under the impact.

"Think they've had enough?" Sewell fired another long burst from the mini-guns, tracking from side to side on a ten-degree pivot, five degrees off center.

"I'd say we can send our goons in now." Ross hit the switch by his knee, and a trolley sent a rope ladder descending toward the ground. He turned to the sergeant in charge of the Asians with all the heavy weapons. "Good luck," he said. "Take out as many of the jerks as you have to, but try and save me some prisoners, okay?"

The Vietnamese, a bright smile across his dark face, gave the thumbs-up and unleashed a torrent of directives at his men. They rushed toward the ladder, many jumping on it even before the bottom rung had reached the jungle floor—they were eager to participate in their first firefight beyond the Cambodian border.

"Looks like it's smooth sailing from here on in," Ross said, pointing down to the edge of the smoke cloud at the base of the limestone cliff. Arms raised in the air, the bandits were filing out into the open.

Sewell patted the cyclic between his legs. "I'd say Dragonfly Numba Three done convinced them to surrender, Roscoe. Them clowns were dumb . . . but not *that* dumb."

Ross nodded his head in submission, and blew a kiss at the control panel. "Thank you, baby. . . ." He patted the thin skin of the ceiling above them and shifted the flak jacket about under his haunches. "Now all you gotta do is take us back to Saigon. . . ."

Sewell kept the craft hovering in a stationary position for several more minutes as they watched the task force on the ground round up the leaders of the opium-smuggling gang.

The Vietnamese sergeant in charge, his rifle in the back of the young man who had taken Lu-long's place as kingpin, glanced up at the Huey and formed the "all's well" sign with his fingers.

"Okay," said Ross. "Score one for the round-eyes. . . ." They would now wait for the head Chinaman to be escorted back up into the chopper along with his lieutenants. Four fellow renegades, to be exact. An equal number of task-force troopers would remain behind on the ground—the chopper could only carry so many passengers—to keep an eye on the kingpin's followers, and to destroy the stockpiles of opium inside the caves.

"What's next?" a voice in the back of the helicopter spoke for the first time since the mission had left Saigon.

Ross glanced back over his shoulder at Mr. Tri. "As soon as everybody's back on board," he said, "we'll beat feet over to Princess Raina's camp. They've got a clearing large enough there for Matt to set the Fly down. We'll have a friendly little talk with our prisoners and decide which are most likely to accept new leadership."

"And those that won't?" Tri interrupted. Ross was glad the congressman had taken his advice and remained behind, safely in Saigon.

"They will be handed over to the authorities in Phnom Penh."

The Huey gave only the slightest hint people were climbing up a ladder into its open hatches—it dipped from side to side as each new person grabbed onto the ladder—and then Collins was giving the thumbs-up and securing the cable winch.

"Take her up," the lieutenant said, turning to survey the anxious faces of his prisoners; it was clear they had never seen a helicopter up so close, much less ridden in one. Their terror kept them subdued better than handcuffs. Ross wondered how long it would last.

"Don't worry," Sewell read his thoughts. "If they give us any shit, we'll teach 'em how to dog paddle without a parachute!"

Colonel Parker roared as he lunged forward, jabbing Chandler in the stomach with his iron fist. The NVA officers cringed, and their shoulders tensed as the American vomited onto his chest.

The big German stepped backward in disgust,

wiped his claw against Chandler's face, then yelled again and plunged the steel fingers into his belly a second time. This time he grabbed the American's insides, however, and started to twist. Chandler threw his head back and screamed at the top of his lungs.

The ex-mercenary hung from the ceiling of the interrogation cubicle, his wrists attached to long chains by tight manacles. He was unable to resist.

"Your name!" the German yelled. To this point, he had given no hint that he had recognized the man he had sold weapons to, long ago and far away, on the dark continent of Africa. To Big Chad, Vietnam was beginning to look a lot darker than Rhodesia. "Your name!" Parker repeated, twisting in the other direction.

"Rafferty!" the American finally replied.

The name did not have the effect on Parker Chandler had hoped it would—a slight twinkle in the German's eyes perhaps, but nothing else.

Rafferty was the Australian who had insulted Parker beside the campfire, calling him a Nazi kraut.

"Your entire name!" The interrogator pushed in hard with the claw, until Chandler thought he could feel the iron rubbing against his backbone.

"Chakka Rafferty, you son of a bitch!" Chandler brought his head back up and spat at the German. Parker responded with a vicious backhanded slap that nearly tore the American from his suspension chains.

"Leave us!" Parker whirled around to face the two North Vietnamese officers. The captain was holding his stomach—he looked like he himself was on the verge of throwing up.

"But—" the major started to protest mildly.

"I must be alone... to concentrate," Parker explained impatiently. "My interrogation methods are a science it has taken me years to develop... *leave the room!*"

Hoping to save face, the major took his subordinate's arm, as if to assist him out of the chamber.

"Give me one hour with the bastard," Parker added, "and I will have from him all the information you desire...."

"Very well." The major waved his free hand in resignation as he shut the door quietly behind him. "One hour...."

Parker's expression changed completely after the door closed. He slammed his fist down against the desk top a couple times, but he was winking at Big Chad the entire time. He waited a couple minutes, then checked the door with his ear. He cautiously opened it and peered down the hallway outside in both directions.

"I think we're alone now," he said, his accent disappearing as he returned to Chandler and began loosening his bonds.

"So you remembered me," the ex-merc sighed, looking down at the red welts rising on his belly.

"From the instant I saw you," Parker smiled. He tapped Big Chad lightly against the bruises on his stomach. "But we had to make it look good, didn't we, my friend? These Orientals are not easy to deceive."

"You did an excellent job." Chandler doubled over painfully as the wrist manacles came off.

"Last time I saw you, you were leading a team of cutthroats across the badlands of Mozambique headed for a bank heist...."

"Some slight... complications arose over that caper," he responded. "I'm just as surprised to see *you* in this part of the world. Still running guns?"

The German raised his hands as if surrendering. "Now I didn't ask you what you were doing in Vietnam, did I?"

"But you are obviously helping me escape." Chandler breathed in a lungful of the damp air as his ankles were freed. "This will put a quick end to your 'Interrogator' activities—"

"Which have only lasted a couple weeks, my old friend. The 'legend' behind this... claw here," and he raised his hand in front of Chandler's face, "was fabricated... passed from village to village in this region by word of mouth. My people paid some neutral villagers to spread the story that a big fat East German with a claw on the end of his right arm was coming down the trail from Hanoi. You're the first round-eye I've gotten to use my hardware on...."

"Nice workmanship." Chandler was rubbing the soreness from his joints—he still could not walk. "Made in Salsbury?"

"Bombay." Parker grabbed a steel ashtray with the metal fingers and crushed it. "Fuckin' Indians will design anything if you've got the greenbacks or diamonds to pay for it.... And what am I doing in this lousy sewer drain, you are dying to know? Well, I'll tell you this much, Mr. Chandler: the Commies got a big cache of guns hidden in these hills. I've been chasing down leads for months... *and I want it!*"

"So you can sell them to somebody else."

"You're catching on, son. And why do I risk my skin helping you?" Parker had two holsters on his belt and he unsnapped the rain flap on the one over his right hip. "Because this morning I found out, from one of the double agents they let me interrogate, just where those big guns are . . . and I just might need some help from friendly forces.

"*You* happen to be friendly forces," Parker continued. "But something tells me you're still free-lancing, and your friends—if you've got any—are in the kind of outfit the American government would never officially claim responsibility for. . . ."

"Therefore," Chandler said wryly, "we might look the other way while you pile the big guns into a convoy of trucks and race off for the black market in Laos."

"You're smart enough to be a fucking ossifer." Parker handed him one of the pistols, butt first. "Now let's excuse ourselves graciously from this pitiful excuse for a party. . . ."

"How much ammo you got on you?"

Parker frowned and handed him five more magazines.

"I've got a buddy that's going along with us." Chandler was telling the German, not asking.

Parker glanced out the door into the corridor again. "Fine," he sighed. "The more manpower, the better our chances of bluffing our way outta here. Can he walk?"

"He's in great shape," Chandler smiled, and they started down the hallway toward Pruitt's cell.

The North Vietnamese major felt his face turning

red. "You embarrassed me back there, *Lieutenant*," he told the officer who had been a captain only moments before. "You have worked at this center nine months, yet today you grow faint merely because we are privy to a new method of interrogation. This afternoon I will have your transfer papers ready for your signature...."

The lieutenant sat bent over in a bamboo chair, trying to hold down his stomach. He had become sick not because of the German's demonstration with the American, but because he had supervised the question-and-answer session with the accused double agent the day before. During that interrogation, Parker had gone further than just twisting the man's belly about.

The big man had forced his iron claw completely through the prisoner's stomach, tearing out his intestines with one swift jerk of the arm. The session culminated, he had then thrown the entrails at the NVA officer and stormed from the chamber, laughing uproariously. The lieutenant had grown nauseated today because he was anticipating a repeat performance.

"I understand, Major." He felt his head clearing. "I will cooperate fully. I am sorry if I embarrassed you...."

"Be sure to send me a postcard from Lao Kay," the major said, slamming the door behind him as he left the office. Lao Kay was a settlement on the Chinese border that had been receiving increasing cannon bombardments from radicals in the Red River Hills.

The major checked his Rolex—a souvenir from a

Green Beret he had ambushed outside Pleiku some months earlier—and frowned. Only fifteen minutes had passed since he'd left the East German.

"Nonsense!" he grumbled to himself, pacing back and forth at the entrance to the corridor which led down into the heart of the interrogation center. Who is in charge here? he asked himself. It is you, fool! his pride told him, and he began a speed march toward the cellblock where he had left The Claw with the stubborn American.

"Get to your feet!" Chandler leaned into Pruitt's dark cell and motioned for the lieutenant to hurry. "It's Independence Day!"

"I *knew* you'd get us out of here," the air force officer said, slapping Chandler on the back, "I just *knew* it!" But he skidded to a halt outside his cell when he came face to face with the big German.

"We've got to get those ankle manacles off him," Parker pointed out. "We'll never make good our escape otherwise."

"Who's this guy?" Pruitt fought off the urge to raise his fists defensively.

"An old friend," Chandler said without elaborating. Then, to Parker, he said, "The key's not on this ring," referring to the holder the guards left on a nail at the entrance to the corridor.

Pruitt stared at the awful-looking claw on the man's hand. "The major keeps the ankle keys on his belt," he said. "The handcuffs keys too."

"Back into the cell," Parker told him. "We can't be found lollygaggin' around out here." He clicked the metal fingers of the claw together loudly, staring down at the chain between Pruitt's ankles. "Let me see what I can do about the problem."

"Who exactly are you?" the airman asked a few seconds later, as Parker worked on cutting through the manacles.

The German glanced up at J.P. and stared thoughtfully into his eyes for a moment. "You might say I'm an international adventurer, of sorts," he boasted. "From Peking to Panang, Seoul to Singapore . . . I've swindled the goods out from under the best of 'em. . . ."

"Jonathan Pruitt." The young pilot held out his hand.

Parker did not immediately take it. "Pruitt. . . ." he muttered, throwing all his energy into cutting the chain. "Knew a Pruitt long ago . . . back during the war . . . damned good man. . . ."

J.P.'s eyes lit up. "The war?" he asked, mouth open even after the question was out.

"Korea."

"Sgt. Johnny Pruitt?"

Parker's steel fingers grated to a stop and he looked up at the kid again, but didn't say anything.

"He was my father!" Pruitt said. "*Is* my father. . . ."

"Was, son," Parker corrected him. "I'm sorry . . . I'm really sorry." He went back to working on the manacles as a diversion from the emotional scene that was developing between the two men. "I hope we're talking about different people. . . ."

Pruitt's shoulders fell as the hope drained from him. "We are talking about the same person," he said slowly. "Please tell me what you know about my father's disappearance."

"The Chinese captured him at an outpost called Camp Starburst." Parker began. "He was badly wounded. They turned him over to the North Koreans, who promptly charged him with war crimes. He refused to sign a confession or cooperate in any way. They executed him seventy-two hours later. His body lies in a mass grave on the Chinese border...."

"Why was my family not told any of this?" Pruitt asked. "My mother went to her grave last year... still not knowing where my father was... whether he was alive or dead...."

"Washington has no open lines of communication with the North Koreans," Parker said. "The information I've just related to you is hearsay... tidbits I've pieced together over the years... clues learned only after a thousand bottles of whiskey with a hundred burnt-out soldiers beside campfires in a dozen different countries. Most of it was related to me by another fugitive of the law... a snake I've had many dealings with—an American deserter, in fact."

"Would he be black by any chance?" Pruitt's face lit up again. "Would his name be Jefferson?"

Parker's face suddenly went white and his eyes grew very wide. His cheeks puffed out slightly, as if he'd taken in a breath and decided not to let it out.

"Lift your hands above your head," a deep voice with a Vietnamese accent cracked the hushed silence, as the NVA major pushed the pistol farther into Parker's back. "Very slowly."

The German did as he was ordered, and as he stepped back out of the cell, Pruitt could see that the small Vietnamese officer meant business. Pruitt's head did not move, but his eyes darted about beyond the Asian whose pointed cap came up only to Parker's shoulders.

"Where is the other prisoner?" the major demanded.

He got his answer sooner than he expected.

As he had taken the German by surprise, a wire cord flashed past his eyes from behind. The garrote swung against his throat, and before he could fire his pistol, the major was jerked off his feet as the cord sliced through his larynx to the vertebrae.

"Surprise!" Chandler's head appeared behind and slightly to the side of the gurgling Vietnamese. He had been waiting back in the depths of his own cell the entire time the major had been sneaking up on Parker. Flexing his massive biceps, he jerked the garrote tight one last time, then shoved the limp body into the conex behind him and kicked the door shut.

"There!" Parker had gone down on one knee again and had finally cut through the ankle chain. He jumped back out of Pruitt's cell, eyes darting up the corridor. It still appeared deserted. Retrieving the major's automatic, he asked, "Which way do you want to make our 'dramatic' departure?"

"There's only one exit out of this corridor," Chandler said. He pointed up at the shafts of light at the end of the hallway, where the major's office was located.

"Then we'd best quit wasting time," Pruitt muttered.

* * *

The demoted captain's head rose slowly from between his legs. He wiped his moist eyes, forcing visions of the Lao Kay border settlement from his mind, and concentrated on the only door into the major's office.

There it was again! Two more shadows shot past the crack at the bottom of the door.

He holstered the pistol he had just been holding against his temple and rose to his feet, reaching for the doorknob.

"Halt!" He brought the front sights of the weapon down onto the big German's back and jerked the trigger before giving the fleeing trio time to respond. The high-caliber slug slammed into the crease between Parker's shoulder blades and blew him off his feet.

Chandler whirled around from right to left, pulling the trigger repeatedly throughout his turn.

Five slugs tore large splinters from the pillars supporting the roof, and the sixth struck the lieutenant in the center of the chest. He was catapulted backward off his feet into the office from which he had just emerged.

"Run in there and retrieve his weapon!" Chandler ordered young Pruitt as he went down on one knee beside Parker.

"Right!" the air force pilot nodded, heading for the doorway now slick with a pool of blood.

Chandler forced his fingers into the big German's wound, probing. "It looks bad," he said, not wanting to lie to the man.

Parker closed his eyes and groaned. His forehead moved slightly up and down, acknowledging what the American had just said.

"Where is the cache?" Big Chad's lips brushed up against the gunrunner's ear. "Where is the cache of heavy weapons?" Already, footsteps could be heard running toward their position.

Parker forced his lips apart and told Chandler twelve numbers, map coordinates, an effort he completed only with great difficulty.

Chandler ran the numbers through his mind, but shook his head angrily. He did not think he would be able to remember them all in the correct sequence.

He raised his pant leg and grabbed Parker's claw. There was no time to search the major's office for a pen or pencil.

After he had carved the coordinates into his calf, he brought his lips back down to Parker's ear again. "Thanks buddy . . ." he said, "I'll see to it somebody somewhere builds a monument to your memory . . . we'll fire a twenty-one-gun salute, using the weapons from *this* cache!" and he slapped his calf, ignoring the sting.

"Let's go!" Pruitt flew out of the major's office, another pistol in his hands. "I've got it!"

"You know what you must do," Parker said, his words coming out slurred and laced with blood.

Chandler frowned, but nodded his head.

"Let's *go!*" Pruitt's face was tense.

"But first. . . ." The big German rolled painfully onto his side and began struggling with the appendage hanging from his right arm. He finally twisted the claw off and held it up in the air between them. "Take this with you," he said, handing the monstrosity to Chandler. "I'd be rolling in my grave for eternity if I knew the bloody Commies got a hold of it...."

"They don't allow people like you and me the luxury of a grave...." Chandler muttered. Shouts and directives in Vietnamese could be heard growing in the distance now.

"I know...." The man with no country sighed, rolling back over onto his stomach.

"Come on!" Pruitt's eyes were wide with anticipation.

Chandler slowly stood up, chambered a round into the German's other pistol, then aimed it down at the back of the man's head and smoothly pulled the trigger.

12.

When the women threw dry palm fronds onto the bonfires the flames shot up several dozen feet. Ash floating on the warm evening breeze glowed yellow and orange, and threatened to set the rain forest afire as it swirled up through the dense triple canopy. But the celebrations had never gotten that far out of hand yet. And the mist rolling in with midnight kept the leaves and bark moist.

Ross sat around one of the half-dozen campfires with his team, silently watching the festivities . . . nursing his flask of rice wine. Even Cory was keeping a low profile, leaving the girls alone. They danced only with men of their own kind tonight. This was a Khmer celebration.

Rising up behind the vast clearing the Cambodians had come to call home, was a longhouse on stilts. It had been built in record time: three days, after word of the Americans' successful mission had reached camp and it had become clear the valleys of Svay Rieng would now be at peace.

Lanterns glowed inside the far end of the dwelling, where Rollins and his people were showing Mr. Tri which laws he would have to follow in order to receive the monthly allotments of aid from the U.S. government. Lieutenant Ross and the War Dogs had elected to pass up the briefing. The congressman from Massachusetts had flown in by helicopter at the last moment to bask in the glory of the victory so many of his associates back on Capitol Hill had maintained could never be won. Ross felt his people were not paid enough to stomach the lengthy speech Stubbs was bound to give. They would much rather enjoy the food and drink outside, where they could watch the topless maidens dancing between the raging bonfires.

Excitement danced in the eyes of the War Dogs also as they observed the festivities, but few of them wore any smiles. Somehow they all felt guilty... or unfulfilled—like the mission hadn't really been a success at all. Perhaps it was the fact they also felt loss. Tonight there was one less War Dog among them. And they had not even been able to lay Chandler's body to rest.

Young Cory was the first to notice that perhaps the Americans in that jungle clearing weren't the only ones feeling reserved... even a bit depressed. Many of the Khmer men sat in tight circles, talking quietly, ignoring the music. And leave it to Cory to notice something different about the breasts of the dancers.

The tips of their breasts are not jutting out, he told himself, squinting at the golden bodies as they glided by on the breeze. They're flat and listless, when they should be erect... taut. These girls are not aroused by the music like they've always been before. They're not putting their hearts into the dance!

Even Collins and Sewell could feel it. Brent was sure it had something to do with the arrival of Congressman Stubbs. The Khmers of this tribe were jungle dwellers. They were highly superstitious—even their princess, who had been educated in Europe. The night signified danger to them, it was the unknown, home to evil spirits that flew into hiding when the dawn returned. Stubbs was the first black man they had ever seen. To the Khmers, he was something to be feared. After all, he *had* dropped in through the trees, so to speak—totally uninvited. In Collins's eyes, the congressman was the personification of all that was evil, and that's how he felt the Cambodians saw him.

"We must talk to you."

Ross glanced up to find Princess Raina standing in front of him. Amy was by her side. Pok-kal, the princess's brother, was behind them, several of his followers clustered around him. Serious expressions masked all their faces.

"Is it so important it can not wait until the morning?" Ross directed his question to Amy. "Now is the time to relax . . . to party. . . ."

"I think you'd better listen to what we have to say." Her eyes were icy and her jaw was set firm.

Rollins ran his skinny fingers back over his bald crown, wiping the sweat off, then pushed his wire-rim glasses up the bridge of his nose. His headache was getting worse. And now they were beginning another round of laughter that would run a couple minutes before the joke was totally translated among the Vietnamese and Cambodians in the room, who would "get" the punch line late, and laugh some more. This was supposed to be all business, the company man was fuming, but all we've heard for the last two hours were Stubbs's ethnic jokes. . . .

"My, my!" The congressman rocked back in his chair and patted his bloated belly. "I haven't laughed this hard since the Democratic National Convention!"

Mr. Tri passed him another platter of steamed shrimp. "If we could get back to business for just a minute," he insisted. "I would like to go over the section about profit sharing again—it seems rather vague. . . ."

"Profit sharing!" Stubbs acted like he was about to choke on the chicken bone in his mouth. "This is the middle of the jungle, my friend! Why do you even *need*—"

"If we could just go over a few points," Tri interrupted, pulling the notebooks back out of a briefcase. "It will only take a minute or two."

"If you'll promise to tuck one *or two* of those slender almond-eyed maidens under my covers tonight!" Stubbs pointed down to the girls dancing around the bonfires outside, then slapped Tri on the back. It appeared that the congressman planned on staying the night. "And make 'em cherry-girls, boy! *Cherry*-girls!"

"Yes," Tri frowned at the physical contact and the disrespect toward the girls outside. "Cherry girls. . . ."

"After all," Stubbs continued, "you are in charge of this . . . *encampment* now, my friend. And there's a lotta *love* children running loose out there—no, make that love *slaves!* Yes, I like that term better: *love slaves!*"

Several of the men in the room exchanged irritated looks but said nothing.

"If we could just get back to this item on page five," Tri said, flipping through the notebook.

A hush fell over the room just then. Stubbs's smile faded, and Tri, sensing trouble, whirled around to face the doorway.

Justin Ross had entered the longhouse, arms folded across his chest.

On either side and slightly behind him stood Collins and Sewell. Both men were armed with M-60 machine guns.

As if conditioned to respond this way in times of stress, Congressman Stubbs's smile returned, brighter than ever. "Ah, Lieutenant Ross," he said. "Welcome to my castle! Come in! Come in! I thought I had missed you . . . I thought perhaps you had gone back to Saigon. We were just . . . *inaugurating* Tri here, so to speak, into his new position of authority. . . ."

Ross locked eyes with the congressman, but Sewell and Collins had been staring at Tri the whole time. The Vietnamese shifted a few steps behind the politician from Massachusetts.

"So I see. . . ." Ross said softly. "Let me offer my congratulations!" He grinned as he started toward the grim-looking man with the notebook in his hand.

When he was a few paces in front of Stubbs, Ross swiftly drew his pistol from its holster and rested it against Tri's forehead.

"Good luck in your new position!" the army lieutenant muttered. He pulled the trigger and Tri's head flew back, a purple crater where the front of his skull used to be. The man's body flopped onto the floor, and his feet began kicking the congressman's chair.

Nobody in the room moved.

Except Stubbs. "My God, man! What have you done!" He bolted across the room, wiping blood and bits of brain matter out of his hair. The chair he had been sitting in tipped over backward onto what was left of Tri's face.

"Shut up, Stubbs," Collins shifted the muzzle of his M-60 so that it was against the congressman's belly.

"Are you people crazy!?" the congressman yelled. "Have you all gone mad!? What is going on here? What have you done?"

"Yes. . . ." Ross slowly holstered his pistol and sat on the edge of the desk. His eyes never left Stubs's now. "What *was* going on here?"

"I don't know what you're talking about, *Lieutenant!*" Stubbs stared at the blood on his hands incredulously. "I'll have your commission for this! Your commission, *hell!* I'll see you behind bars in Leavenworth before this is all over!"

"I don't think so." Ross's death's-head grin erupted across his grim features.

"You're living in a dream world, Ross!" Stubbs pointed his finger at Collins's team leader, and the ex-policeman knocked it down with the M-60 barrel. The congressman glared at Brent, but remained frozen to the spot. "You people are all mad!"

"I wonder what your associates back on the Hill will think when they learn the head of the anti-drug investigative committee is one of the biggest dope pushers in the Orient," Ross said.

Stubbs laughed uneasily and broke the stare-down contest. "You're not talking about me, my friend...."

"I wonder what your associates will think when they find out Congressman Stubbs recruited Mr. Tri there," Ross pointed down at the corpse at his feet, "a long-time underworld drug trafficker, to take over operations here along the profitable Cambodian-Vietnamese border region, so that money from the opium harvest could go to Congressman Stubbs's campaign machine instead of some illiterate Chinaman living in a limestone cave deep in the rain forest...."

"You'll never in a million years prove *that* one, Ross!" Stubbs pointed his finger at the lieutenant again, batting Collins's machine gun away this time. Ross signaled the team's sniper not to retaliate.

"It's no secret your party has high aspirations for you someday," Ross said. "I've even seen editorials in respected magazines that predict you might reach the White House in your lifetime. Campaigns of that intensity and duration take money, Stubbs . . . a lot of money...."

"You're talking out your asshole, Ross!" Stubbs threw his chin out, like a street tough bluffing a rival gang member. "You're spoutin' theory and conjecture that wouldn't stand up to a Saigon breeze in a court of law!"

"Speaking of Saigon," Ross's smile grew, "I've got a whole roomful of files, Congressman Stubbs. And in the last few weeks some other people interested in your background have discovered a few jewels I'm sure the world would love to hear about."

Beads of sweat were breaking out on the politician's forehead.

"It seems you've got a few skeletons in your closet, kind sir. . . ."

"I don't have to stand here and listen to this!" Stubbs tried to brush past Collins, but the ex-policeman swung the stock of the machine gun around and clipped the congressman's jaw, knocking him off his feet. He slid across the pool of blood collecting beside Tri's deformed head, coming to rest in a corner of the room.

"That felt good," Collins whispered over to Sewell. "Just like being back on the street, just like engagin' in some good ole stick-time. . . ."

Sewell nodded and smiled back, but didn't say anything.

"You're not going anywhere, Stubbs," Ross announced. "Unless it's with a pair of handcuffs on your wrists. . . ." The lieutenant pulled a set of the metal bracelets from his belt and dropped them in the congressman's lap. "Put them on," he said.

"I will not!" Stubbs responded indignantly. "Why should I?"

Ross chuckled with satisfaction, happy to hear the question, and he glanced around the room. Everyone was frozen to the spot, devouring every word of the confrontation. Princess Raina and her followers had appeared in the doorway. "Because you are not Leon

Stubbs at all, Mr. Congressman, but one Leon *Jefferson*, United States Army deserter!"

A gasp swirled through the room.

"And this business with the opium and the taskforce cover isn't even your primary reason for venturing way out here into the sticks, is it, Stubbs . . . or Jefferson, or whatever your name is?"

The congressman gritted his teeth, rage boiling in his eyes, but he didn't say anything.

"Somehow you got access to the War Dogs file," Ross continued, shifting his gaze onto Rollins. "I'd wager this weasel here tampered with the computer at the Big P or something and found out about our rather unconventional methods of eliminating enemies of the government. You've been leading a double life of sorts these last thirteen years, Mr. Stubbs-Jefferson: running up and down the length of Asia, passing secrets to the Communists, slipping through the congressional background checks somehow to rise that political ladder until you arrived at where you are today.

"But a problem arose a couple years ago, didn't it?" Ross's eyes returned to the congressman's. "A young air force lieutenant started getting too close to the truth, if I've got my cards laid out right. The son of the man you betrayed thirteen years ago on a Korean battlefield was suddenly hot on your trail, and through Rollins here, you threw a wrench into the Green Machinery and succeeded in putting a hit out on young Pruitt. It just wouldn't have done to let the world find out Leon Stubbs . . . *Congressman* Leon Stubbs fell asleep on guard-duty thirteen years ago, only to detonate a mine that killed several fellow

Americans when he was rudely awakened by a U.S. recon team crawling back to camp with their wounded. *Then* Congressman Stubbs deserted his post without raising the alarm after the Chinese launched a surprise attack. All of Camp Starburst was wiped out because of Congressman Stubb's sense of self-preservation, but did the politician grieve?" Ross turned to look at the people in the room like a prosecutor facing a courtroom full of spectators. "*No!* While his fellow Americans froze in the blizzard or perished under the onslaught of Communist bayonets, our dear congressman was sitting snug in a warm interrogation booth, sipping wine with the Chinese!"

"*Lies!*" Stubbs rose to his feet and shook his fist at Justin Ross. "You just murdered the man sanctioned by the U.S. government to lead these people from a life of illegal activities to a more productive and rewarding existence, and I will not rest until I see you and your team of cutthroats prosecut—"

"*This* man is the true leader of the Svay Rieng Khmers!" Princess Raina held the bamboo drapes hanging in the doorway back, and her brother entered. "Only *he* can lead our people through the difficult times ahead." The princess, radiant in royal robes Ross had never seen her wear before, stepped closer to Stubbs, but stopped as the pool of blood spreading across the floor almost touched her feet. "And I can see by what has transpired here tonight, now that white men . . . and *black men* have come to our valley, we are indeed in for difficult times ahead. . . ."

The young prince stepped over the body of Tri and

brushed the notebooks off the desk, into the blood. "We no longer need the assistance of the United States," he said, looking directly at the congressman. "And we no longer shall fight with the opium smugglers." He stared across the room at what were left of Lu-long's lieutenants. They bowed their heads respectfully. "You, Mr. Congressman," the prince glared at Stubbs with restrained fury, "may now leave my kingdom. Never come back."

Stubbs shook his fist at Ross. "You have not heard the last from me!" he screamed.

A loud discharge shattered the tense stand-off in the room, and Congressman Stubbs toppled backward over the desk, his chest heaving in and out where the pistol round had slammed through his sternum.

Ross and the others turned to see Big Chad Chandler standing in the doorway, the NVA major's pistol in his hand, smoke floating in front of the barrel.

"I'd say we *have* heard the last from you, Leon-honey," he said. Collins's cemetery chuckle sliced through the heavy silence.

Chandler stuck the pistol down inside his belt and slowly walked over to the wounded congressman. He went down on one knee and ran his fingertips along the edge of the beard until he found the scar.

It was the gash he had inflicted on the sentry thirteen years earlier. "It's him." Big Chad rose to his feet and walked back out of the room without saying anything else.

Stubbs, wheezing painfully from the sucking chest wound, rolled his eyeballs in relief and looked at the hostile faces surrounding him, searching for compassion.

They froze when they came across the towering frame of Air Force Lieutenant Jonathan Pruitt. The pilot was holding Collins's M-60 now, and the muzzle was pointed at the congressman's face. "Don't . . . do . . . it. . . ." Stubbs pleaded, his jaw shaking violently now.

Pruitt hesitated, then his frown broke into an ear-to-ear grin. Stubbs smiled, too, and started laughing, but then he understood, and the terror returned to his face.

"This one's for Dad," the airman muttered softly, and he pulled the trigger until the long belt of ammo hanging to the floor had disappeared.

EPILOGUE

There was a panther in the trees just beyond the string of bonfires surrounding the Khmer encampment. It was screaming up at the moon as Chandler stepped out onto the balcony of the longhouse. *Just like Africa*, he mused, basking in the mood that was the jungle closing in on him. *I can hear her, but I can't see her....*

After the staccato rattle of gunfire from inside the longhouse had died away, and a fine misty drizzle had begun to fall across the rain forest, Chandler turned to find young Cory MacArthur running up the steps to greet him. "Big Chad!" the kid screamed joyfully. "We thought you were dead! Welcome back, brother! Fucking welcome back!"

Chandler, though he was far from in the mood, held his arms out to let the charging soldier embrace him. "Thanks, Cory... it feels good to be home...."

"Lotta stuff been goin' on around here, Chad," an embarrassing smile creased the kid's face. "Lotta things have changed...."

"That young Cambodian girl I was sharin' a

stretch of beach with still around?" Chandler asked.

"Yep," Cory swallowed hard, "she's still around...."

"Then tell me about all the news tomorrow," he replied. "Save the gossip for sunrise. The best favor you can do me right now is lead me down to the love of my life and the woman of my dreams!" He slapped Cory on the back, and arm in arm the two War Dogs started back down the steps of the longhouse.

"Okay, Big Chad... follow me!" MacArthur's head bobbed from side to side with anticipation. "Have I got a surprise for you!"

THE BEST IN ADVENTURE FROM ZEBRA

THE ZONE #1: HARD TARGET (1492, $2.50)
by James Rouch
Across the hellish strip of Western Europe known as The Zone, supertanks armed with tactical nuclear weapons and lethal chemicals roam the germ-infested terrain. War in the mist-enshrouded Zone is a giant game of hide and seek — with a deadly booby prize for the losers!

THE ZONE #2: BLIND FIRE (1588, $2.50)
by James Rouch
In a savage frenzy of blood and fire the superpowers fight the Third Battle of Frankfurt. American Major Revell must delay a Communist column — but only a madman would take on Shilka anti-aircraft tanks with outdated mines and a few Dragon rocket launchers!

THE WARLORD (1189, $3.50)
by Jason Frost
The world's gone mad with disruption. Isolated from help, the survivors face a state in which law is a memory and violence is the rule. Only one man is fit to lead the people, a man raised among the Indians and trained by the Marines. He is Erik Ravensmith, THE WARLORD — a deadly adversary and a hero of our times.

THE WARLORD #2: THE CUTTHROAT (1308, $2.50)
by Jason Frost
Though death sails the Sea of Los Angeles, there is only one man who will fight to save what is left of California's ravaged paradise. His name is THE WARLORD — and he won't stop until the job is done!

THE WARLORD #3: BADLAND (1437, $2.50)
by Jason Frost
His son has been kidnapped by his worst enemy and THE WARLORD must fight a pack of killers to free him. Getting close enough to grab the boy will be nearly impossible — but then so is living in this tortured world!

Available wherever paperbacks are sold, or order direct from the Publisher. Send cover price plus 50¢ per copy for mailing and handling to Zebra Books, Dept. 1647, 475 Park Avenue South, New York, N.Y. 10016. DO NOT SEND CASH.

FAVORITE GROSS SELECTIONS
by Julius Alvin

GROSS JOKES (1244, $2.50)
You haven't read it all—until you read GROSS JOKES! This complete compilation is guaranteed to deliver the sickest, sassiest laughs!

TOTALLY GROSS JOKES (1333, $2.50)
From the tasteless ridiculous to the taboo sublime, TOTALLY GROSS JOKES has enough laughs in store for even *the most* particular humor fanatics.

UTTERLY GROSS JOKES (1350, $2.50)
The best of tasteless, tacky, revolting, insulting, appalling, foul, lewd, and mortifying jokes—jokes so sick they're UTTERLY GROSS!

EXTREMELY GROSS JOKES (1600, $2.50)
Beyond the humor of gross, totally gross, and utterly gross jokes there is only the laughter of EXTREMELY GROSS JOKES!

GROSS LIMERICKS (1375, $2.50)
This masterpiece collection offers the funniest of rhythmical rhymes, from all your favorite categories of humor. And they're true-to-form, honest-to-goodness, GROSS LIMERICKS!

GROSS LIMERICKS VOLUME II (1616, $2.50)
Rhyming limericks so bold, sassy, and savvy they'll leave you laughing right through the night with delight!

GROSS GIFTS (1111, $2.50)
It's the Encyclopedia Grossitanica, with everything from gross books to gross cosmetics, and from gross movies to gross vacations. It's all here in the thoroughly and completely tasteless and tacky catalogue we call . . . GROSS GIFTS!

Available wherever paperbacks are sold, or order direct from the Publisher. Send cover price plus 50¢ per copy for mailing and handling to Zebra Books, Dept. 1647, 475 Park Avenue South, New York, N.Y. 10016. DO NOT SEND CASH.

THE BEST IN ADVENTURES FROM ZEBRA

GUNSHIPS #1: THE KILLING ZONE (1130, $2.50)
by Jack Hamilton Teed
Colonel John Hardin of the U.S. Special Forces knew too much about the dirty side of the Vietnam War—he had to be silenced. And a hand-picked squad of mongrels and misfits were destined to die with him in the rotting swamps of . . . THE KILLING ZONE.

GUNSHIPS #2: FIRE FORCE (1159, $2.50)
by Jack Hamilton Teed
A few G.I.s, driven crazy by the war-torn hell of Vietnam, had banded into brutal killing squads who didn't care whom they shot at. Colonel John Hardin, tapped for the job of wiping out these squads, had to first forge his own command of misfits into a fighting FIRE FORCE!

GUNSHIPS #3: COBRA KILL (1462, $2.50)
by Jack Hamilton Teed
Having taken something from the wreckage of the downed Cobra gunship, the Cong force melted back into the jungle. Colonel John Hardin was going to find out what the Cong had taken—even if it killed him!

THE BLACK EAGLES #4: PUNGI PATROL (1389, $2.50)
by John Lansing
A team of specially trained East German agents—disguised as U.S. soldiers—is slaughtering helpless Vietnamese villagers to discredit America. The Black Eagles, the elite jungle fighters, have been ordered to stop the butchers before our own allies turn against us!

Available wherever paperbacks are sold, or order direct from the Publisher. Send cover price plus 50¢ per copy for mailing and handling to Zebra Books, Dept. 1647, 475 Park Avenue South, New York, N.Y. 10016. DO NOT SEND CASH.

A TERRIFYING OCCULT TRILOGY
by William W. Johnstone

THE DEVIL'S KISS (1498, $3.50)

As night falls on the small prairie town of Whitfield, red-rimmed eyes look out from tightly shut windows. An occasional snarl rips from once-human throats. Shadows play on dimly lit streets, bringing with the darkness an almost tangible aura of fear. For the time is now right in Whitfield. The beasts are hungry, and the Undead are awake . . .

THE DEVIL'S HEART (1526, $3.50)

It was the summer of 1958 that the horror surfaced in the town of Whitfield. Those who survived the terror remember it as the summer of The Digging—the time when Satan's creatures rose from the bowels of the earth and the hot wind began to blow. The town is peaceful, and the few who had fought against the Prince of Darkness before believed it could never happen again.

THE DEVIL'S TOUCH (1491, $3.50)

The evil that triumphed during the long-ago summer in Whitfield still festers in the unsuspecting town of Logandale. Only Sam and Nydia Balon, lone survivors of the ancient horror, know the signs—the putrid stench rising from the bowels of the earth, the unspeakable atrocities that mark the foul presence of the Prince of Darkness. Hollow-eyed, hungry corpses will rise from unearthly tombs to engorge themselves on living flesh and spawn a new generation of restless Undead . . . and only Sam and Nydia know what must be done.

Available wherever paperbacks are sold, or order direct from the Publisher. Send cover price plus 50¢ per copy for mailing and handling to Zebra Books, Dept. 1641, 475 Park Avenue South, New York, N.Y. 10016. DO NOT SEND CASH.